Breaching

The

Walls

Breaching

The

Walls

The story of three lives–three men who served years together in the eastern Pennsylvania prison system. One made the best of a bad situation and was finally released. The other two made the worst of it, thinking only of their freedom. In the end, one escaped the law and the other used the law to escape.

Joseph J. Corvi

and

Steve J. Conway

Cover photo provided by Eastern State Penitentiary Historic Site. Cover design by Tom Mullin.

ISBN 0-9725468-0-4
Library of Congress Control Number 2002095857

For additional copies of this book, contact:

Personal Legends Publishing
50 Chapel Hill Road
Media, PA 19063
610-565-8705

Printed in the U.S.A. by
Morris Publishing
3212 East Highway 30
Kearney, NE 68847
800-650-7888

DEDICATIONS

To Warden William J. Banmiller, who lent new meaning to the term rehabilitation and gave purpose to inmate education and training.

To James "Botchie" VanZant: he was sustained by his humor, strengthened by his courage, and driven by his perseverance.

To Frederick "Saint" Tenuto: a fearless adversary and stalwart friend who ultimately triumphed over the system and stayed free.

Table of Contents

PROLOGUE

On April 3, 1945 the headlines in the *Philadelphia Inquirer* blared, "Fleeing Convict is Shot; 10 Others Trapped in Passage Under Wall." Stories on succeeding days described a spectacular escape through a hand-dug tunnel nearly 100 feet long. Most of the escapees were captured rather quickly. All were desperate criminals–two murderers, three serving life sentences and, except for one, the remainder all long term convicts. Among the most famous was Willie Sutton, the self-proclaimed escape artist and notorious bank robber. Finally, when the dust settled only two men remained at large, Freddie Tenuto and James Van Sant.

Frederick J. Tenuto, also known as Saint, carefully closed the apartment door behind him and stood on the stoop at the top of the stairs, looking around with feigned casualness. Satisfied, he descended the steps and, thrusting his hands into his trouser pockets, walked briskly down Amsterdam Avenue, turning onto Broadway. Within two blocks he entered Hennessy's Taproom, waved offhandedly to the bartender and joined another man at a table toward the rear of the room. The second man, who was already seated at the table with a glass of beer in front of him, was Michael Quinn. He was in his shirt sleeves, but wearing a tie. A navy-blue, double breasted suit coat hung over the back of his chair. He smiled and nodded as Tenuto took a seat.

The two men exchanged words as the bartender brought a Yuengling beer and placed it in front of Tenuto. "Where's your buddy today?" the bartender inquired of nobody in particular, just making small talk. His attempt at friendly banter was ignored. As he left, Tenuto raised his glass in a toast to Quinn and took a sip. Then he replaced the glass in front of him and, ignoring his companion, gazed into the foamy head like it was a crystal ball. It was late May and beginning to warm up in New York City's West Side. Tenuto was a small man at only five feet five inches, but had a stocky build. At the moment he was smiling, a trifle lopsidedly, and thinking back.

The two holdouts had managed to elude the authorities with the help of Mike Quinn, also a wanted man it turned out, who provided the two fugitives with money and groceries and a safehouse in New York City. Quinn had been a big help, but now they were running out of cash. It was time to make a bank withdrawal. Tenuto wasn't worried about the prospects in the least. Armed robbery was his business–at least when he wasn't serving time. His reveries were interrupted when another man entered the restaurant.

James Franklin Van Sant, also known as Botchie, was only slightly taller than his partner in crime and about the same weight. Like Tenuto, Botchie had been serving time for armed robbery before the escape. The difference was that while Botchie had shot a man during a holdup, Tenuto was convicted of second degree murder. In actual fact, both men had committed numerous armed robberies over the years.

Van Sant joined his two friends at the table. After a third beer had been delivered, the men began to talk quietly about a bank robbery they'd planned for the next day. In fact, the robbery was supposed to have happened on this very day, but Saint got himself drunk last night and was too hung over to carry out the plan. After reviewing the plans briefly and satisfying themselves that all was in readiness, they began to study their menus with the care of men who were still unaccustomed to the novelty of choosing a supper of their own liking, instead of look alike, taste alike, smell alike prison fare.

So engrossed were the men in making their selections that they all failed to notice two newcomers enter the room. They walked right up to the table where their prey sat contemplating a fine meal and drew their weapons. One of the two said, "Stick 'em up; we've got you."

"You got us," Quinn exclaimed as he threw his hands up. "Don't shoot!" Although all three of the criminals were armed with revolvers, they wisely kept their hands in plain view. No sense arguing with drawn guns pointed and at close range.

The two Philadelphia police department detectives, Richard Doyle Jr. and Arthur Henningsen, had been searching for the two escapees since the breakout had occurred nearly two months ago. A week earlier they'd enjoyed a bit of good luck when they received a tip as to the fugitives' whereabouts in New York City and had teamed with some of New York's finest to close in. While the men were being watched, always separately, they were seen in the company of another ex-convict who owned an automobile. It was thought that the men were casing a New York bank. Today was the first time all men were found in the same place and at the same time. Their arrest foiled another robbery.

Quinn, who had been at large for some time, was wanted for several armed robberies and questioning regarding three murders. Van Sant was serving 10 to 20 years for shooting a liquor store clerk during a holdup. Tenuto was under a 20 to 40 year sentence for robbery and second degree murder. All three criminals waived extradition and on the day following their capture were on their way back to Philadelphia under close guard. This wasn't the first prison escape for the two men, nor would it be their last.

Chapter 1

Young Joe Corvi

Making a living, even living itself, was tough in the United States during the depression years. Early on, on that infamous black Thursday, October 24, 1929, and during the following days, bankers, financiers, and wealthy investors, full of despair and totally without hope of ever recovering their lost fortunes, were leaping out of tall building in New York City. Those were the years (between 1929 and 1939) of soup kitchens in the cities and hungry children and hobos riding the rails, scouring the country in search of work, and the Works Projects Administration and a rising crime rate as men sought alternative means of providing for their own and their family's needs. There was nowhere in the country where the effects of the Great Depression weren't found.

Fate dealt a lot of kids a bad hand during this period, but not Joe Corvi. He readily admitted that he was the architect of his own misery. Corvi was growing up in South Philadelphia at the time, living on the 2400 block of Rosewood Street with one brother and three sisters. His mother died when Joe was six years old and the kids were raised by their father, Venanzio Corvi. The kids were infinitely more fortunate than most. The elder Corvi was head chef at Philadelphia's premier restaurant located in the Rittenhouse Hotel on Rittenhouse Square and never missed a day's work. Consequently the Corvi family, while they may not have been living off the fat of the land, never really wanted for much either. Their home on Rosewood Street was a nice red brick affair with three bedrooms. The family always ate well, and the kids all had at least the same stuff as all the other neighborhood kids.

At age sixteen Joe was a sophomore at Southern High School and was getting excellent grades even though he rarely did any homework. He had a nice looking girl friend, Emily, who he took out for a soda or a "Talkie" once in a while. He was mostly polite–always to adults–and dressed neatly. Joe, unlike most of his friends, always had a little money in his pocket. Anyone who knew young Joe, and was asked, would probably have said, "He's a good kid, stays out of trouble, and doesn't sass his elders."

As a matter of fact, he seldom even cursed unless seriously provoked by some action or event. Instead he used a phrase he picked up at burlesques–like the Bijou Theater which was located on 8th Street and Race and the Trocadero over on the edge of China Town. The slap-stick comics, such as the Slats and Scrapple team that were popular in Philadelphia at the time, seldom used foul language during a performance. Instead, wherever a curse word was appropriate, the comic would substitute the phrase, cheez and crackers. That's cheez as in jeez and crackers as in saltine. Corvi began using that phrase as a substitute for foul language at a young age and continues to this day even though the term is extinct.

The young man did have one serious defect, however. He possessed sort of dual personality, a Jekyll and Hyde complex. He lived two lives. His alter ego was a thief, a burglar actually. He never did a job in his own neighborhood, for the simple reason that nobody there had much worth stealing anyway. Nor did he pilfer items like the family silver, phonographs, or bulky items like that. Instead, he favored something he could secret in a pocket and innocently walk down the street with. He prospected in the richer neighborhoods–where the money was, so-to-speak.

Joe didn't need to steal. He had a bicycle to get around on, his clothes weren't ragged, and he regularly got a little spending money from his father. In other words, unlike a lot of kids, Joe was in no way deprived. Maybe the problem was he had too much time on his hands. He didn't need to study much, if at all, and his father worked long hours, so Joe had nobody at home asking where he was or what he was doing. Later, asked for an explanation for his extracurricular activities he said, "It was the challenge of doing the job and the thrill of getting away with it."

Over an eight month period Joe did five burglaries. In his spare time, he wandered around the wealthier sections of town, like Chestnut Hill or Lancaster Avenue, looking for the right patterns–regular departures and arrivals, extended absences, and the signals suggesting a house without people–clues such as darkened windows when there should be lights, an accumulation of newspapers, or the absence of an automobile in the driveway. If all the signs were lined up right, Joe payed the house a visit. And, in general, he did well. He spent the loot on himself, but not conspicuously. That is, he didn't suddenly appear with new clothes or flashy jewelry, just a little spending here and a little there.

Job number six was the residence of William S. Vare, a well known, wealthy, and formidable senator of Pennsylvania. The target residence was generally occupied only on weekends and appeared to be an easy trick. After a couple of weeks of reconnoitering and planning, it took only minutes to get in and out of the house with one pocket full of cash and the other with some rich looking jewelry–rings and necklaces and stuff–all of which was found in the master bedroom suite. Just being it that room was an experience. He'd never seen anything quite like it. There was a floral wallpaper that he couldn't resist feeling; it felt silky to the touch. The draperies were heavy and likewise had a soft feel. The massive furniture was ornately carved and glistening with oil, like it had been freshly polished. There was even a fireplace and it must have worked because there was a neat little pile of wood on the hearth.

Joe was so impressed with the room and satisfied with the loot that he was tempted to leave the good senator a gracious note complementing him on his excellent taste and thanking him for the personal contribution. It was a nice haul and he should have quit while he was ahead. Instead, several days later he returned for seconds. Joe had just finished rummaging around the bedroom, picking up some overlooked jewelry, when he heard voices downstairs.

There was a large cedar chest in the bedroom and Joe managed to squeeze himself into it with some difficulty. There he stayed for about an hour, remaining hidden until he had heard no further noise. Cautiously, he lifted the lid to the chest and peered out. Nobody was in view and he heard no talking. With caution, he crept down the stairs that had some alarming creaks and navigated through the house to the back door. He glanced out the door onto the back porch and beyond, seeing nothing. Confident now, he slipped outside and headed across the porch. As he approached the steps a voice from behind him said, "Where da ya think you're goin?"

The young thief's heart almost leaped right out of his chest! He didn't think to run. Instead he turned, with a start, in the direction of the voice. The voice continued, "Throw up your hands, pal. You're under arrest." He'd walked right into the arms of a police officer who had been sitting quietly on the porch, waiting for the house to get secured. Had he left by the front door, he'd not have been caught. Joe didn't give the cop a hard time or any sass. His only reply was, "Yes sir." Under his breath it was "cheez and crackers."

———

The judge took a dim view of Joe's "other life" and decided to teach him a lesson. He was sent to Huntingdon Reformatory, along with 20 other miscreants, for an indeterminate period to contemplate his sins and, hopefully, become rehabilitated. The reform school was located in Huntingdon, Pennsylvania, in the north central part of the state, out in the State College, Altoona area. The legal system didn't waste any time getting the newly adjudicated young men on their way. Twenty-one young criminals boarded a train and spent several hours in blissful ignorance, singing songs and otherwise acting like teenagers, under the watchful eyes of five deputy sheriffs. They actually had a good time singing their way across the state–songs such as *Just a Gigolo*, *Star Dust*, and *Stormy Weather* (Remember the Movie of the same name starring Lena Horne?). *Stormy Weather,* was a favorite and, perhaps, unconsciously prophetic:

"*Don't know why . . . there's no sun up in
the sky, stormy weather . . .*

Life is bare . . . gloom and misery everywhere, stormy weather . . . ."

At the end of each tune the lot of them would applaud wildly while laughing uproariously at their own performance. Maybe it was the honest laughter of some kids just having fun, like children on their way to summer camp, or, perhaps, the nervous laughter of men facing uncertainty and the unknown with some amount of fear and trepidation. Who knows? Maybe they were making the best of the situation and like Joe Corvi, "Taking it in stride."

The deputies seemed to enjoy the performance, probably as much for the incongruity of the scene as anything else. Undeniably, there was some talent present. Joe, the tenor of the group, had a good singing voice and harmonized well. One of the officers, name unknown, said to Joe after one particularly good performance, "Hey, kid, we should take ya back ta Philly with us. Maybe ya could sing at some of our parties." The cop paused for a moment and then added, "Hell, maybe I could be your agent." Then he laughed.

Joe replied, "Oh, I'd like that. I'd like that a lot." That really brought a chuckle. "I'll bet ya would."

———————

At Huntingdon the inmates disembarked and were taken by bus to their "new home." This leg of the trip was relatively quiet. The situation was about to become reality and each inmate kept his own counsel. There wasn't a sound as the bus turned into the long drive approaching the prison. And that is what it really was–a prison. Everyone craned his neck to see what the place looked like. Words like, "damn," or "Jesus Christ." broke the silence. What it looked like was formidable, like a dark, foreboding, mediaeval castle. It was an old structure even then, with brick walls that seemed impossibly high. The entrance was through a single, stout wooden door with heavy iron hinges. Past the door there was a long hallway covered with a domed ceiling. Footsteps clattered utterly without rhythm along the hallway as forty odd feet moved with jostling independence. At the end of the hall was an iron, dull-black barred gate.   Joe Corvi thought, *this ain't goin to be no bed a roses*. He wasn't wrong.

———

If Joe had known anything about the Pennsylvania Penal System or the Pennsylvania System, as it was called at the time, he probably would have been more than a little concerned. Although Huntingdon was built of brick, its architecture and operating philosophy was exactly the same as the infamous Eastern State Penitentiary in Philadelphia.   The American prison system, as it existed in 1933, had its inception in 1829 with the building of Eastern State Penitentiary in Philadelphia and was the brainchild of the Quakers who thought that inmates could better be rehabilitated through a combination of strict segregation and religious meditation. The theory was that a convicted criminal couldn't be rehabilitated if he was allowed to associate with other criminals. Thus the inmates were completely segregated from each other with no interpersonal contact allowed–ever.

Huntingdon's system wasn't quite as strict and confining as that found in Eastern State during the early days, but, as Joe discovered, it was a difference only of degree. After the normal check-in procedure and the standard physical examination, every new inmate was issued two pair each of trousers, shirts, socks and underclothes. In addition, each man received one pair of black, high-topped shoes–prison issue, prison made.

There were five cell blocks at Huntingdon. Four, A through D, radiated from the center like the spokes on a wheel. Again, similar to Eastern State. E-Block, an addition necessitated by a steadily increasing inmate population, was an extension of the original A-Block. The hub of the wheel was the control center. Access to the cell blocks was through the hub. It was where the guards mustered for duty and it was the place where prison justice was administered every day. Following a perfunctory orientation, all of the "guests" were taken to their new homes in B-Block. Home was a cell about 8-feet long and 5 1/2-feet wide. The narrow bunk was constructed of an angle-iron frame with a lattice work of thin steel bands to serve as support for the mattress. A small wooden chest was supplied for clothes and personal gear. The only other amenity was the "hopper," a cast iron, cone shaped receptacle located in the corner to the left of the door which served as the toilet. On the hopper rested a pail that was used as a wash basin. There was a single faucet directly over the hopper (and the pail) which served a dual purpose–to carry away the human waste and to fill the wash bucket.

When Joe arrived at his cell he found a single blanket, two sheets, a pillow with pillow case, and a single towel. There was also a mattress of sorts, a shapeless lump of cotton ticking that was filled with straw. As Joe would soon discover, in order to use this prehistoric piece of bedding, the lump was beaten until it flattened out somewhat. From that point on it would conform to the body's shape while it was slept on. He stood in the doorway to his cell, looked at the small pile of clothes he was holding in his arms and studied the bunk with the lumpy ticking. Then his eyes took in the space that defined his living quarters. Forty-four square feet containing only the bare necessities. *It's sure no Rittenhouse Hotel,* he thought. He entered the cell, turned, and looked out. The view wasn't much better that way. He thought of the lyrics of the song: "... Life is bare, ... gloom and misery everywhere."

———————

The daily routine at the reform school was bare bones simple. Up at 7 o'clock for the morning ablution and constitutional. The inmates urinated into the hopper standing up, the other required a squat. Washing was accomplished by half leaning and half squatting. The pail was too low to comfortably lean into and too high to squat. They didn't make anything easy in this place.

At 7:30 the doors clanged open. Everyone stepped out into the aisle and lined up according to height–tall guys in the front of the line and short to the rear. With everyone in order, all marched to the mess hall under the watchful eye of the ever present guards. After breakfast it was back to the cell for a short time, until the 8:30 work call. The inmates worked five days a week from 8:30 to 3:30 with a short break for lunch. The prison was self-sufficient to some degree. There was a captive powerhouse for electricity, hot water and heat; all cleaning and maintenance were done by inmates. But the main industry was building furniture–desks, table, and chairs–for all the state offices. Joe eventually wound up working on the steam pumps in the power house. Initially, however, he was moved around. It was on lawn detail that he first really learned about reformatory discipline.

———————

Mr. Lindsay was the guard/supervisor of the grounds. Joe and several other inmates were raking and trimming and mulching the border of the hedge lining the perimeter of the buildings. In the process an inmate had carelessly stepped on the freshly mulched area and left a footprint. The guard, who was quite fussy, inspected all work in great detail. When he spotted the footprint, the outrage welled up into his chest. He glared at the offending indentation and then looked around at his help until his eyes fell upon Joe Corvi. The reasoning was simple: Joe was big, the footprint was big, therefore Joe was the culprit.

"Corvi," the guard almost screamed, "get over here."

Cheez and crackers. Joe snapped to attention and came at a trot, not having any idea what was wrong, but knew he didn't like the sound of the guard's voice. At last he stood erect before Mr. Lindsay. "Yes Sir," he said.

There was no preamble and no questioning. "Look at that," the guard snapped angrily. "Haven't you got any better sense than to walk in the damned flower beds?" Clinching his fists, he continued cursing and sputtering and raving at poor old Joe.

Joe didn't exactly know what to do, but he did know he didn't step in the bed. He also knew he'd better be careful. "Sir, I'm sorry, but I didn't do that."

"What da ya mean ya didn't do it? Who the hell else's got feet that big?"

By now Joe was losing his temper a little. Justifiable, but not too smart. "Hell, I don't know, why don't ya call em all over here and look?" Joe said with a little edge in his voice.

"Don't sass me, Kid. Hell, there's a time I'd a slapped the shit out of ya for sassing." Lindsay was getting all puffed up and red in the face.

Joe felt compelled to respond. "There was a time I'd have slapped ya right back!"

That did it. Within minutes Joe was standing in front of Mr. A. B. Sutherland, the Deputy Warden of the institution (also called deputy superintendent or D.S.), listening to Lindsay angrily describe how this damned kid had smart-mouthed him. A. B. was a big, square jawed hulk of a man who tolerated zero lip from anybody, especially inmates. His speech was gruff, as was his behavior. As his size and behavior might imply, Sutherland was also a bully who worked in a place where nobody could do very much about it.

The D.S. stood there, in front of Joe, his beefy hands grasping the lapels of his coat and looking very stern. He listened carefully to the complaint with narrowed eyes as his stern demeanor transformed into something more closely resembling rage. Joe watched and listened to all this happening in disbelief. He knew he had been out of line, but this was no capital offense. When Lindsay finished, Sutherland's right hand came straight from his shoulder in a blur of motion, hitting Joe square in the face and knocking him backwards several feet before gravity overtook him. Ears ringing and blackness closing in on him, Joe managed to get back on his feet. "Put him in segregation. We'll decide what to do with him later," snapped Sutherland.

The segregation cells were all located on one tier of C-Block. They were the same size as the regular cells, but there was no bunk, no bench, no anything, just the bare floor and the hopper. There wasn't a blanket either, so the inmates slept on the concrete floor, all cuddled up with themselves trying to keep warm. In cooler weather, they never did get warm. While in the cell, there was no contact with anyone except the guard who handed over the single daily meal on a tray. During the daylight hours the inmates were assigned to the scrub gang, punishment work.

The next day Joe had a hearing, once again with Mr. Sutherland presiding. The D.S. had a desk on a raised podium which was located over the guards' locker room. Each offending inmate stood before him, hat over his heart, and received his sentence. In Joe's case it was the scrub gang. The scrub gang was well defined, but the sentence length indeterminate. Only Sutherland knew how much time an inmate would serve and the time was pretty much at his whim and pleasure.

Labor on the scrub gang involved scrubbing cell block floors, on hands and knees, with a heavy deck brush. The inmates stayed on their knees for the entire eight hour days–no meal served, no rest, and no toilet breaks. If nature called during the day, an unavoidable fact of life, the inmate had to ask permission, which was not always directly forthcoming. When the guard finally did grant the boon, a plain old galvanized bucket was used in a most embarrassing way. If number one was the problem, the pants were unzipped, the inmate exposed himself to the world, and leaned over the bucket hoping that nature and the various organs would cooperate, which was not always the case. For some, it was utterly impossible to function with everyone watching. If the delay was prolonged, as happened at times, the guard would take away the bucket and order the boy back to work. This was not a negotiable command. For some, shortly after being ordered back to work, the urge would become impossible and they would urinate in their pants.

If the problem was number two, and everyone knows the sphincter muscle can hold things back for only so long, the kneeling position was still maintained, but legs were spread to allow for the bucket to be brought close enough to rest the backside over the rim of the bucket. In either case, the experience was debasing, embarrassing, and inhuman treatment–all in the name of rehabilitation.

It would seem like the conditions, the work, and the "functional" experience would be enough to encourage entirely exemplary behavior. However, there were a good many of the boys–incorrigible trouble makers, social misfits, and the mentally unbalanced–that were consistent inhabitants on the C-Block and the scrub gang. However, one didn't have to be a major trouble maker to be sentenced to floor work. The behavior that would land an inmate in the scrub gang could be quite trivial. For instance, talking in line, horse play, or being caught with contraband, such as an extra bar of soap all warranted a misconduct hearing. And, if a person managed to get on the wrong side of Officer Dore, one the guards, that was sufficient in and of itself.

Dore was one of those people who was simply mean and ornery–all the time. When there was nothing to become angry about, he'd create something. For some reason, Dore seemed to take special pleasure in harassing Corvi. On Saturday mornings the inmates were required to thoroughly clean their cells. That included washing out the hopper and scrubbing the floor. Joe was a fastidious fellow and kept his cell in apple pie order at all times, so it seldom required much time to tidy things up. On one occasion Dore came by and spied Joe sitting on his bunk reading a book. This looked like shirking to him and he ordered Joe to scrub his floor. Joe looked up and said, "The floor's clean, Mr. Dore. My cell's always clean." Wrong thing to say.

Dore stalked off purposefully. Minutes later he returned with a bucket full of dirty water and threw it into Joe's cell. The cells weren't very large so one bucket managed to cover most of the floor's surface. "It's not clean anymore," he said with obvious satisfaction. "Now, scrub the floor."

On another occasion Joe was called up before Mr. Sutherland for misconduct. The charges were read and the question asked: "Guilty or not guilty?" Joe's question was, "Who lodged the charge?" Officer Dore had for some reason lodged the complaint the day before, a day during which Joe had never even seen the man. It did little good to argue the case. Excessive denial or personal defense would just earn you more time on the gang. Back into segregation he went and the next day he was scrubbing the floors.

In a way, getting off the gang was almost as bad as being on it. Each day, at the end of the shift, A. B. Sutherland made a practice of reviewing the crew. They would line up in a single long row, hat held in the right hand over the heart. Mr. Sutherland would make his way down the line and interrogate each inmate gruffly: "What did you do?" The inmate would answer and then one of two things happened. Sutherland, always with his hands at the ready, would feint a punch to your face. If an inmate attempted to protect his face, Southerland would hit him in the solar plexus, otherwise he got it in the mouth. And, Sutherland never pulled a punch regardless of an inmate's size. This was all done to the great amusement of the attending screws. The up side of this physical abuse was release from the scrub gang and the right to return to your regular cell that night. Failure to get punched meant the return to segregation and to the scrub gang on the following day.

———

There wasn't much about Huntingdon to recommend it. It was a mean, inhospitable place for the young inmates. Some even feigned mental illness in order to escape in the hope of being transferred. Joe recalled one time when he was on the mop detail–mopping the halls and corridors of the cell blocks and administrative buildings–and became ill enough to be excused from work. A replacement was assigned to fill in for Joe. The replacement was sent to the storage room, along with a new crew member, to pick up Joe's equipment. While at the storage room, the new crewman picked up a hammer and beat the hell out of the other fellow, causing severe head trauma. The attacker was diagnosed as mentally ill and sent to Farview, an insane asylum located in Waymart, Pennsylvania. This was an unfortunate ploy since many inmates sent to Farview never were released. It turned into a life sentence.

A prisoner who behaved as described above, or one who assaulted a guard–some egregious violation–was given either a sanity or punishment hearing. The result generally was a transfer to Farview, as in the former case, or another penitentiary. In any event, while the arrangements were being made the inmate was "stored" in solitary confinement which was located in A-block. The cells were the normal height, 8-feet, but were otherwise minuscule in size. They were triangular with a hypotenuse of about seven feet. That meant the sides were less than five-feet long–not much larger than a good sized closet. This tiny enclosure was really empty, not even a hopper, just a slop bucket. The cell was equipped with a latticed steel door constructed of two inch wide steel straps. In addition, outside the steel door there was a solid wooden door that slid on a track. When the wooden door was closed, the cell was thrown into darkness. The only light was when the guard very briefly opened a small hatch to hand in food.

Normally, the minimum confinement was seven days. For the first three days the inmate received one piece of bread and a cup of water each day. On the fourth day he would begin receiving one normal meal per day, usually the evening meal, until he had served his time.

The conditions at Huntingdon were such that some inmates deliberately chose to attempt getting transferred to another prison in the system. One of particular interest was Graterford, a new prison about 30 miles outside of Philadelphia that, compared to Huntingdon, was said to be like a country club. That was probably an exaggeration, but it was deemed to be far better than the reform school. The thought was that if an inmate continued to misbehave long enough, he might be transferred. Some were actually successful, others weren't. One of the latter was Freddie Tenuto.

Chapter 2

The Saint

It was at Huntingdon that Joe met Frederick Tenuto, also known as Saint or St. John. His nickname came from the period of time, at age eleven, that he spent in St. John's Home for Boys. Apparently he had been committed because he was always running away from home and managed to be constantly in some sort of trouble. The school administrators should have taken heed because the young boy escaped from St. John's shortly after he arrived, staying only long enough to acquire the name. Saint was already in the Huntingdon population when Joe arrived and was maybe 17 or 18 years old. The crime for which Saint was imprisoned at such a tender age? Armed robbery.

The two boys were from South Philly, although they had never met and had grown up in entirely different circumstances. In fact, they never did become good friends–just acquaintances in a closed society. But this wasn't strange at all. Saint had few, if any, friends. For one thing, his looks, rather like those of a coiled rattlesnake, did not encourage advances–friendly or otherwise. Saint has been described as swarthy looking, with jet-black hair and piercing black eyes that could bore a hole right through you. At the same time he was quiet, expressionless and inclined to keep to himself, not inviting any sort of interaction. If he was standing right next to you, along with some other young men, you probably wouldn't even remember seeing him. Anonymous, that's the word. He was anonymous. This combination of characteristics, both the menacing features and the anonymity, might have been contrived–nothing more than a strategy for protecting himself in a population of young males with raging hormones. Corvi thought this might be the case until one Saturday afternoon out in the yard. The Saint could take care of himself very nicely, thank you.

On Saturday afternoons, after their cells were rendered sparkling clean, the inmates were allowed out into the yard. There they could find pick-up ball games, sparring matches and other activities. It was there that the boxing team, under the tutelage of an assistant coach named Zender, could be seen doing bag work, skipping rope or sparring. Joe was sitting in the bleachers watching the fighters with interest. There was Tenuto, whose stature was diminutive–he was only 5 foot, five inches tall and appeared slender in the normal prison garb. However, stripped to the waist for a boxing match, a sturdy musculature was revealed. He was actually in the lightweight class at the time, but even as he grew older probably never weighed much over 140 pounds or so. Not that weight made much difference in a place like Huntingdon. You fought all comers from featherweight to heavyweight. It didn't seem to make any difference to Tenuto, who, in any case, behaved a lot like a cobra killer–a mongoose.

His chin tucked in and gloves up, close to his face, Saint would slowly, but gracefully, advance across the ring at the sound of the bell, black eyes glittering over the top of his gloves. He'd fix his opponent with an almost hypnotic stare until he was within range. Then the little Italian would unleash a flurry of combinations–left jabs and hooks–that would open up a man's defense like a meat cleaver and leave him vulnerable to heavy blows to either the face or the body. His attacks were measured, furious and relentless. Most opponents wouldn't last more than a round, or perhaps two. They were either knocked out or simply failed to return at the sound of the bell. When an opponent was knocked down, Tenuto would back off as required and wait, watching the downed man intently, waiting for him to pull himself off the canvass for some more punishment.

Corvi thought this swarthy, dark-haired young man with the deadly, riveting eyes and explosive power could really be a force in professional boxing. Of course, what did he know, being just a kid himself. Apparently the rest of the inmate population felt the same way. Nobody messed with Tenuto. As for the athletes, every

Saturday afternoon, weather permitting, they sparred, a sort of informal elimination process. On Sunday there were the games and everyone who could would be in the bleachers watching. Tenuto never lost a fight.

Tenuto may have enjoyed his pugilistic dominance but out of the ring he kept his nose clean for the most part, remaining characteristically invisible. Nobody escaped the Scrub Gang, but he seemed to have minimized the unpleasant experience. None of this meant he enjoyed the place. He wanted out, desperately, just like everyone else, but there was one major problem with the system. All sentences at Huntingdon were indeterminate. An inmate's actual sentence was determined by the institution's staff board. The minimum sentence was eleven months. At that time there was a hearing during which the board would convene and, depending upon your institution record, your crime, and your behavior, make a determination. The board might allow parole in eighteen months or twenty months or twenty four months. And whatever the sentence, it could be extended for up to six additional months if an inmate committed some misconduct or more serious infraction that seemed to warrant additional punishment.

If a parole was granted, three months before his scheduled release the inmate was permitted to contact family and friends and send them a set of parole papers which would identify where he was going to live upon release, where he would work, and who his sponsor would be. This plan, once returned to prison administration, would be submitted to the parole authorities for verification. If the plan was accepted the inmate could be released on the predetermined schedule except as noted above. In most cases, if everything was in order, an inmate would be released within a week or so of the scheduled time. There were, however, exceptions to this rule and Saint was one of them.

Mr. J. P. Snare was the institution's Parole Officer and, for some reason–perhaps it was Tenuto's withdrawn behavior, which could be interpreted as a certain surliness, or perhaps it was his original crime, which was more serious than most–Snare decided that Tenuto wasn't yet completely rehabilitated. He had exhibited no remorse. Maybe that was the problem, he had exhibited no emotion at all. Saint had given the parole letter to Snare, who was supposed to mail it to the appropriate parties and then make a judgment of the responses' worthiness. Weeks passed before the parole candidate became a little impatient. He went to Snare's inmate clerk, a young man named Nugent, to see what was going on.

"Hey, Nugent, my papers were sent out a long time ago. Kin ya tell me if they've been returned yet?"

"Yeah, they been returned. Snare's got em." Nothing more was offered and finally
Tenuto turned and left with a shrug.

After several more weeks passed without word, Tenuto returned to Snare's office and again asked the question. This time Nugent entered Snare's office, opened a file drawer, and pulled out a file. Waving the file at Tenuto, Nugent said quietly, "This is yours. I don't know what the hold up is, but your papers have all been returned and seem to be in order." Dejected, Tenuto returned to his cell. He had a choice, make an appointment with Snare to see what the problem was or try to talk with A. B. Sutherland, the Assistant Warden. He decided that talking to Snare would not be a good idea. If he lost his temper, he'd be in some kind of permanent trouble. Instead, he went to Sutherland.

The Assistant Warden tried to be helpful, which was unusual. To Tenuto's query he said, "The papers may have been misplaced. Might be a good idea for you to submit another plan."

Tenuto hesitated a moment, thinking over the pros and cons of telling Sutherland that he knew the papers were in Snare's filing cabinet. Finally, he decided to tell Sutherland without involving Nugent. "Mr. Sutherland the other day I went to Mr. Snare's office. Nobody was around so I went to the filing cabinet and looked for myself. My papers are all there, sir."

Sutherland looked at him in disbelief. In short order, Tenuto found himself being escorted to a solitary cell in A-Block. And there he stayed for three days before receiving his first meal other than bread and water. In four more days he was brought before Sutherland on charges. Snare, himself, came to A-Block to escort the inmate to the hearing place at the hub. While they were walking out of the cell block Snare turned to Tenuto. "What's a matter, Freddie, don't ya like it around here?" he said nastily. "Ya need to get something through yer head, kid, I say if and when ya get out a here."

When the pair arrived before Sutherland, he looked stern and fixed Tenuto with a baleful stare. "By your own admission, you broke into Mr. Snare's office and rifled his files. How do you plead?" Tenuto looked down at his feet thinking, *I'm had*. "Guilty, sir," he responded quietly. Snare looked on with grim satisfaction.

Sutherland explained, in a severe tone, that breaking into the Parole Officer's office was inexcusable under any circumstances and sentenced Tenuto to labor on the Scrub Gang. He was sent to segregation and spent the next two and a half months in misery. Fortunately, at some point there's an end to everything. Late in 1935 Tenuto was finally released.

Frederick Tenuto returned to South Philly a celebrity, at least among the younger crowd. He had a reputation. He had done time. He was a man to be reckoned with. He also lost no time getting back into the outlawing business and over the next five years went on a one-man crime spree that involved holdups and robberies and one kidnaping.[1]   After all, a guy had to make a living.

When Tenuto wasn't busy "working" he spent his time in the taprooms drinking beer. He especially enjoyed hanging around A. B. Schmidtz's place, a favorite hangout in South Philly. He had a keen taste for brews and also liked hanging around on a street corner with some buddies. The depression was just running down but there were still a great many men, young and old, who had a lot of time on their hands. A fellow corner hanger and one of the few people that Saint called "friend", was Willie O'Niell. One day, when the two men were together, O'Neill confided that he had a beef with a guy and was thinking about killing him.

That declaration sure got Tenuto's attention. "Jesus, Willie, you must be really pissed. What'd the guy do to you anyway?"

"The son-of-a-bitch stiffed me, . . . never mind. I just need ta do em and I need some help. Not killin' em, I just need somebody ta keep the car running so I kin get away quick. Will ya help me?"

Saint only hesitated for an instant. "Sure, I'll give ya a hand. When?"

A plan was made and that evening the pair drove to the Buckeye Club on South 8th Street. Tenuto, who was driving, pulled the car up to the curb and put it in park, leaving the engine running. Willie took a 38 caliber revolver out of his waist band and checked the loads. Then he got out of the car, buttoned up his jacket and crossed the street to the club, which was on the second floor of a large brick building. It was March and still a little cold. Willie walked to the club's entrance with his shoulder hunched against the chill in the air.

Saint leaned back, keeping an eye on the rearview mirror, the street, and the club's door. He smoked a cigarette and then another, tossing the butts out into the street. Finally, Willie came out of the building, not in any hurry, and casually returned to the car. He got in, closed the door, and just sat there staring out the window.

"Well?" Saint inquired.

"Well, what?"

"Wasn't he there?"

"Yeah, he was there. Wasn't right. Couldn't get to him."

"Shit." Tenuto leaned back and just stared at his friend. "Gimme the gun."

Willie looked at him for a moment, pulled the gun out, and handed it over without a word.

Tenuto shoved the gun in his jacket pocket and left the car, heading for the club door. He stopped and retraced his steps. Willie rolled the car window down. "What's this guy's name? What the hell's he look like?"

"Name's Jimmy DeCaro. You'll recognize him easy. He's all slicked up and sitting at the bar. Wearing white shoes."

Saint turned on his heel and walked purposefully to the two story brick building, disappearing through the door. He took the stairs two at time and stopped long enough to spot DeCaro at the bar talking to some other men. Saint walked to within a few feet, pulled the gun out of his pocket and shot him three times in the chest. DeCaro stumbled backwards against the bar and then crumpled to the floor. The normal drone of chatter abruptly stopped and all eyes riveted on the scene at the bar. There was the little man with the glittering black eyes and the smoking gun and Jimmy DeCaro laying on the floor in an ever widening pool of blood. Saint didn't linger, but he didn't hurry either. He just turned around and left, not running, just walking quickly. Back at the car, he got in, closed the door, and turning, tossed the gun in Willie's lap. "Okay," he said calmly, "he's done, let's go."

The murder occurred in March, 1940. In April Saint was arrested and committed to Holmesburg County Prison pending his trial. Eventually he was tried and found guilty, along with Willie. The Saint was awarded a 20 to 40 year sentence, half of which was for being involved in a series of payroll holdups that netted over $25,000 each.[2] He'd been out of prison for less than five years and was now heading back, this time to the real thing. Eventually he was sent to Graterford, that country club prison located outside of Philadelphia. Who's kidding who?

Chapter 3

They Called Him 'Botchie'

James F. Van Sant was brought up in South Philadelphia, or at least that is where he called home. His mother died when he was a young boy and his father, an alcoholic, wouldn't or couldn't take care of the family, so young James and his sister, Isabel, found themselves living with his paternal grandfather on a farm in Maryland. The older man wasn't terribly tolerant of young people, in particular, inquisitive young people. Van Sant was about 13 years old, very active and filled with wonder at all the animals and growing plants he found on the farm. The questions came gushing out of the boy in an endless stream that grandfather considered a grievous assault on his peace and tranquility as well as a scandalous waste of time. For Grandfather Van Sant the solution was simple. Keep Isabel, who was quiet and tractable and could help with the household chores, but send young James back home to his father. The father immediately shunted him off to his brother, Harry, who owned a farm in Delaware.

Harry Van Sant and his wife, Emma, raised produce for the market and, of course, their own table as well. There was all manner of livestock–pigs and chickens, beef cattle and dairy cows, and a black working mule named Thunder. It was just like James' grandfather's place except that unlike Grandfather Van Sant, Uncle Harry took a keen interest in young James, appreciated his inquisitiveness, and encouraged all the questions. So James settled in to farm life, doing chores like feeding the animals, collecting eggs and cultivating the kitchen garden, and attending the local school. In return for the work James received room, board, clean clothes and a good home.

The problem was that he didn't receive any allowance. James had acquired a smoking habit that demanded a bag of Bull Durham once in a while and he liked to shoot a little pool on Saturdays for a nickle a rack, a soda or candy bar was a nice treat too. He had some simple needs, like any young kid, but no money for them. He decided a little pocket money would be just the right thing, so he stole his Uncle Harry's 38 caliber pistol and sold it to a guy in the pool hall. It was, of course, inevitable that Harry would find out about the missing gun and question James about it, and that is exactly what happened. James was ushered into the parlor, which was normally reserved for special occasions, and the interrogation began.

"James, do you know what happened to my revolver?" the older man quietly asked. He was clearly upset and his face looked like a thundercloud. James had never seen his uncle look like this before. He was in big trouble, but really didn't understand what the fuss was about. He felt kind of bad, but, after all, he'd needed some money. He sat there squirming in an uncomfortable chair that was too big for him and looked at his hands for what seemed like a long time, wishing this would all go away. Finally he said in a very low voice, "Sold it."

"But it wasn't yours, was it, James? Why'd you sell it?"

"Needed some money, I guess."

"You needed some money, did you?" Uncle Harry paused. "So you just took my gun and sold it. Well, James, I won't have a thief round the place. You're not to be trusted. Lord knows what you'll steal next. I'm sending you back to your father."

James was silent for a moment. "I'm sorry sir," he said.

"So am I, so am I."

———

James was immediately banished back to South Philly. He never went back to school. For a while he just hung around on the streets, but that became boring, so he found a job working at the John B. Stetson Hat Company. That job was really monotonous, almost as bad and doing nothing, but without the freedom. After all, what teenager would think that sweeping the same floors every day was any fun? One morning on the way to work, James noticed a large poster prominently displayed in the window of an office building. It was a picture of Uncle Sam, complete with top hat and tails and bedecked with stars and stripes, pointing a finger and saying, "I want you!" There was a picture of a battleship crashing through heavy seas. *Now this here's more to my liking*, he thought. He went to the Navy Recruiting Office on 13th and Market Streets and tried to enlist. Of course, the officer in charge knew the young man was too young. "Look, kid," he said, "you get this consent form filled out and signed by one of your parents and I'll sign ya up."

It didn't take long for James to return the form all signed and proper. Of course, he didn't know where his father was, so he'd signed it himself. He was accepted without a hitch and within days was on his way to the Navy boot camp at Great Lakes, Illinois. After the training period was over, he was assigned to the USS Florida and traveled to ports in the Caribbean and the east coast of South America. James loved it and it's hard to tell what would have happened if the ship hadn't been recalled to Newport News, Virginia for conversion from a coal burner to an oil burner. Idleness and boredom were two things that James didn't tolerate very well. He went AWOL to New York City–The Big Apple that lots of his buddies talked about with great enthusiasm and animation. Whether his errant ways were the cause or not, the U.S. Navy chose this time to investigate the youthful recruit's background and found that he had lied about his age. The long and the short of it was that James earned a bad conduct discharge after only eighteen months of service and was, for all intents and purposes, flat broke in New York City.

The Interborough Rapid Transportation Company hired James as an operator/attendant which somehow translated into a job involving the collection of money from the cash boxes into which the riders deposited their fares. It cost one nickle to ride the trolley and it was collected at the turnstile by an IRT attendant who sometimes had to exchange coins for paper currency. The content of the cash boxes was emptied into a heavy cloth bag, picked up periodically during the day and stored, awaiting pickup by a collector car. James worked at Penn Station, which was a very busy place, so there was a ton of money–both silver and bills–stored at any given time. He decided that expropriating some for his own use would be a low risk enterprise. He didn't really give a lot of thought to consequences, didn't think about it at all, just did it.

One day he stuck a revolver he had purchased from a friend for a few dollars into his jacket pocket, stuffed his few belongings into a duffle bag and went to the train station. There he waited and watched the activity in the collection booth until it appeared that a full load was accumulated and all the currency sorted. Then he walked up, stuck his pistol in the attendant's face and left with several bags of money, all he could carry handily in his duffel. To add insult to injury, instead of fleeing the railroad station with the loot as would be expected, he got in a line with a group of travelers waiting to board the Pennsylvania Railroad train heading for Philadelphia.

Once in Philly, Van Sant checked into a small hotel in the Tenderloin section of the city. The Tenderloin was very a rough part of town–the home of prostitutes, pimps, tinhorns and thieves. And, there was five-cent beer. Next door to his hotel was a taproom and it wasn't long after his arrival that James was in that bar with a beer in one hand and an arm draped over the shoulder of a pretty, new female friend. An "arrangement" was quickly made and, after finishing their beers, the young couple started to leave the bar. Before they could get out of the door a very unfriendly looking guy who was as big as King Kong stopped them.

"Hey, Pal, I need some money for a room. Ya know what I mean?"

James looked at this guy and said, "Got a room, right next door."

King Kong hesitated a moment, as if trying to understand what was being said. Finally, he shook his head. "Don't make no difference, ya got to pay me anyway."

It was quite clear that this jerk was in cahoots with Van Sant's girl and intent on robbing him. He probably thought that James was some punk that could easily be trimmed. He found out different. The punk pulled out his gun and stuck it right in King Kong's nose. Actually, it was almost laughable. The bigger man almost appeared to cross his eyes in an effort to watch the business end of the pistol that hovered there, right at the end of his nose. The transformation from gorilla to a meek little mouse was instantaneous and probably the only smart thing Kong had done all day. Van Sant's finger was already tightening on the trigger. Now it was James' turn. He relieved the former tough guy of his money, retrieved the fee from his would be lover, and casually walked out the door. He never even made it back to his hotel before a pair of Philadelphia's finest had him in handcuffs. Hell, all he'd done was rob somebody who was about to do the same to him.

James was booked on a charge of armed robbery and sent to Holmesburg County Prison
to await trial. In the meantime, the Philadelphia police discovered that there was a detainer for him in New York City. In less than three days James Van Sant, who later became known as Botchie because he was always botching things up, had committed two armed robberies, was caught and thrown into jail. At the preliminary hearing, the assistant district attorney elected to drop the local changes in favor of the armed robbery charge in New York, since the latter would carry the heavier jail sentence.

Eventually he was tried and convicted of armed robbery and unlawful flight and sentenced to a term of seven and a half to fifteen years. Initially, he was sent to Sing Sing, which is located in Ossining, New York, supposedly for classification. After five and a half months he was transferred to Dannemora State Prison in the northeastern corner of New York, less than 20 miles from the Canadian border.

Dannemora is actually a little town among dozens of little towns located in the region. The difference between Dannemora and those other towns is that Dannemora is the location of a maximum security prison that houses some of the worst criminals the United States ever hatched. And right next to the prison was the insane asylum, which was commonly referred to as the Bughouse. Some of the particularly nasty inmates at the prison were sent to the Bughouse just for safe keeping, to calm them down and probably to make a point. There, the death rate, from both natural and unnatural causes, was extremely high and generally attributed to suicide regardless of the cause. Convicts familiar with the prison called it Siberia because of the harshness of both the natural environment and the prison itself. In winter the temperatures were routinely sub-zero, sometimes as low as thirty below. Conditions inside the walls were every bit as bad as the weather outside.

One prisoner described the living conditions as "harsh and primitive," and things went downhill from that point. The food was indescribably horrible and boring. Every breakfast was a bowl of mush, a slice of bread and bad coffee. Every supper was half a bowl of soup, a slice of bread and weak tea. Lunch was just as unvarying–nothing–seven days a week, weeks in and weeks out, forever. The bedbugs were so bad you could hear them marching around in the night, and feel them crawling all over you. Some of the inmates tried to smoke them out of the bedding in the evening, but it didn't do any good. An iron bucket with a wooden cover was the toilet in the cells and was cleaned by the inmates in the morning before they went to work. There was no running water in the cells. Twice a day, once in the morning and once at night, each inmate received a very small ration of warm water. Once a week each inmate got a shower, one minute of warm water followed by one minute of cold water. Supposedly, on average, the water temperature was comfortable. The inmates were only allowed to talk in certain specified places. Otherwise, silence was the rule. Upon arrival at the prison everyone was assigned to a job that was non-negotiable and non-exchangeable. Like it or not, this was the job was yours for the duration.[1]

This incredibly inhospitable place became Botchie's home when he was eighteen years old. He described the time he served there as "survival" time. "Being young and not jail-wise, I didn't know enough to go along with the flow. Hell, I didn't even know there was a program to go along with. I was always rebellious, fighting the system and acting the tough guy in order to keep the predators off my back so to speak. Being a bad guy meant not putting up with any crap from anybody. So the first inmate that tried to 'get me,' I creamed with a length of pipe. I mean, I really beat the hell out him. Of course, that earned me some time in isolation, but nobody bothered me after that. The downside of constantly being a bad guy is I was always being written up for misconducts. This equated to time in isolation, and it probably cost me an extra couple of years in prison."

Botchie served six and a half years of his sentence before being paroled to the custody of his father in Philadelphia. The depression was in full swing. There were no jobs to be had and the 24 year old young man was living with his father without two nickels to rub together. No surprise, he decided to take some from somebody who had some and that is just about what he got–a few nickels.

Having just served six and a half years for armed robbery, he decided, again without much thought, to try it one more time. The target was a taxi company, never thinking that they probably wouldn't have much money. After all, during the depression not many people rode in cabs. He walked into the cab company office one night with a borrowed pistol, pointed it at the dispatcher, the only person there, and said, "Open the safe."

"Can't," the burly employee said curtly, "don't have the combination. 'Sides there's no money anyway."

Botchie saw a small metal box on the worn desk. "What's in the box?"

His victim was completely unimpressed by the gun. Either that or he had a death wish. "See for yourself," he said, shoving the box across the desk. While he opened the box, the man continued talking.

"You dumb shit, you ought to rob somebody that's got some money instead of working men who've got damned little." Damned little described the box's contents. There were a couple of dollars in small change but he took it anyway and turned to leave. "Why don't you get a job you lazy little bastard . . . ?"

The man never completed the sentence. Botchie, frustrated by the meager proceeds and angered by the attendant's taunts, turned around and shot him. Then he left the taxi office and, within minutes, ran straight into the arms of a two-man police patrol. The charges were armed robbery and assault with a deadly weapon. The sentence was ten to twenty years in the county prison at Holmesburg. It could have been worse. It could have been the electric chair. He had been on parole for less than three weeks.

───────

Holmesburg wasn't exactly Siberia, up in northern New York, but it wasn't the Hilton either. The Burg, as Holmesburg was called by the men who inhabited the place, was built in 1829 using the same blueprints as Eastern State Penitentiary. It had the same hub and spoke design. Eastern originally had seven cell blocks and that's how many Holmesburg had. From the hub, the guards could see down each block to the end. For the times, the prison had a very efficient communications system–the best available. Those men who, for whatever reason, found themselves in the isolation block, really were isolated. For the term of the punishment, an inmate never left the block except for brief periods of exercise in a tiny, fenced in yard. Nor did the men eat with the population. Meals were delivered to individual cells by a guard.

The worse thing about Holmesburg was the lack of industry, educational opportunities, or attempts at rehabilitation. This place was for short-timers and punishment. If you were serving ten to twenty years, like Botchie, it was an incredibly boring and stultifying and cheerless place. Not that he bitched about it. He knew he'd done it to himself. He didn't like his predicament at all, but he went over six years without making any waves. He minded his own business and did his time. Then during the seventh year he was informed that there was a detainer against him from New York. There was no explanation as to why it took so long for him to find out; it was simply a fact. Translated, the detainer meant that Botchie owed New York nine years after his release from Holmesburg for parole violation. That's when he decided to let himself out of the Burg.

The prison had a farm that provided for some of the institution's needs and was located some distance from the institution itself. The farm didn't require a huge work force and the men that did work there were short-timers, low-risk inmates. The field laborers were transported to the farm by truck. Each morning, the guys bunched up in the yard waiting for the truck to arrive and then everybody clambered aboard simultaneously, trying for a seat on the benches that ran down either side of the vehicle. One day Botchie just became a part of the swarm. Nobody even noticed he was there.

The truck passed through one gate and it closed behind them, enclosing everyone within a 20-foot alley of confined space. Botchie quit breathing and attempted to blend into the surroundings like a chameleon. He needn't have worried. Unaccountably, there was no check, no headcount. Nobody even glanced into the back of the truck. The second gate opened and he could feel the bump as the vehicle passed over the threshold. As the truck merged into traffic, the inmates called out raucously to the passers by and flirted loudly with the girls. Botchie eased himself to the back of the truck and as it slowed in traffic, he leaped to the roadway, stumbled for a second, recovered his balance and raced away. He had just paroled himself!

Holmesburg was located in northeast Philly, maybe a dozen miles from the city center. Botchie hiked across town toward home. Once in the old neighborhood he had no trouble getting a little help from friends–some clothes, a little money, a gun and a place to crash until he could figure out a way to leave Philadelphia. First he needed some more cash, more than he could borrow from friends that were nearly as poor as he was. He laid low for a few days, waiting for the heat to cool, and picked a liquor store on 12th and Spring Garden Street to rob. People would buy booze when they didn't have the money for food. It was a piece of cake. Once in the store, he pointed his gun in the direction of the clerk's ample belly and demanded all the cash. That gun did the trick every time. The clerk couldn't empty the cash drawer fast enough and Botchie was on his way in less than a minute.

He headed to the subway, which was nearby, and took a position on the platform, waiting for a train out of the city. Then he noticed a big guy dressed in worn, baggy clothes watching him. The man's gaze never wavered an inch, just bored a hole in him. Botchie got a little scared and attempted to get away, but the only exit was past the watcher. All he wanted was out of the subway. The guy grabbed at him and got hold of his shirt–a mistake. The fleeing Botchie pulled his gun, shoved the barrel into his ambusher's gut and pulled the trigger. The hand immediately fell away as the man lurched backwards clutching his stomach as he collapsed in a heap on the platform. For a moment Botchie watched to see if the bleeding man was going to stay put and then he became aware of the staring commuters. He ran for the street level, knocking over several arriving passengers in the process.

Once on the street he looked around wildly and spied two men sitting in a car. Out came the pistol and, at gunpoint, the occupants of the car were ordered to leave, which they did with astonishing speed. Botchie clambered behind the wheel and jammed his left foot down in an attempt to start the engine. Nothing happened–silence. The automobile ignition systems had changed since he'd been in prison and he couldn't find it. He was sweating and swearing and frantically stomping the floorboard, sure the starter was there someplace. The rear window exploded inward, shattered by police gunfire. He yanked the pistol out of his waistband and began to swing about to return fire just as the front windshield also shattered, peppering the side of his face with broken glass. He'd had it and knew it. He threw the gun out of the window and himself across the front seat in an attempt to protect himself from further gunfire.

A whole gang of cops grappled him to the pavement. He didn't even remember resisting. Soon, cuffed and shackled, his face a mask of blood, Botchie was rushed off to the emergency room at Hahnemann Hospital. He had severe lacerations, but that was no real problem. The bullet wound in his neck, however, had paralyzed the hapless escapee and bandit from the neck down. The doctor and some nurses were just finished cleaning him up when the guy he'd shot down at the subway was wheeled in on a gurney. Botchie looked at the man, recognized him as his nemesis, and screamed as loudly as he could: "I hope you die, you son-of-a-bitch!" As it turned out, the man was a stock clerk at the liquor store. He had witnessed the holdup and followed Botchie to the subway station.

After a while Botchie was moved from the emergency ward to a private room with round the clock security. The cops, knowing he was paralyzed, didn't pay much attention to the patient. Instead they flirted with the nurses at the desk and relaxed, drinking coffee. Two days later, during a time when the guards were gone, Botchie felt an itch and instinctively began to scratch the offending part. When it occurred to him that he had feeling and could move, he screamed with relief and excitement, "I'm not paralyzed," he hollered at nobody in particular. In seconds the guards crashed into the room, guns drawn and not knowing what to expect. Botchie looked at them dumbly and just thought: *Why didn't I just keep my mouth shut? I probably could've walked right out of here.*

Freedom didn't last very long. In less than a month, most of which was spent in the hospital, Botchie was before a judge again. In 1940 he was sentenced to ten to twenty in Eastern State Penitentiary–that is, along with the remainder of his sentence in Holmesburg plus the detainer in New York. He was now 31 years old, had spent the last 13 years in prison and, by his own accounting, still owed society at least 32 years.

Chapter 4

The Notorious Bank Robber and Escape Artist

After several years of living the life of a thief–safe man, vault man, armed robber–and always living on the edge–William Francis Sutton and friend and accomplice, Eddie Wilson were arrested for breaking into the Ozone Park National Bank in New York City and attempting to burn their way into the vault with an acetylene torch. It was a job they never finished. Wilson, who defended himself, got off scot free. Willie, as Sutton was called, was tried and convicted of third degree burglary and attempted grand larceny. On April 5, 1926 he was sentenced to five to ten years in prison. This was the first major offence for which he had been charged and convicted. Except for a few months in Sing Sing, located in Ossining, New York, awaiting classification, he served the time at Dannemora Penitentiary. He was released on parole in 1929, after serving a little over three years and was twenty-eight years old.[1]

He found himself on the street with a new wife and in the midst of what we now call the great depression. Reminiscent of the similar events described in previous chapters, after spending a little time beating the bushes looking for work, Sutton went back into the robbery business. The first job was the M. Rosenthal and Sons Jewelry Store on Broadway, just a couple of doors south of the Capital Theater in New York City. For the first time, he tried one of the disguise tricks that became his trademark and gained entry into the store posing as a Western Union messenger. He and his accomplice, Jack Bassett, made off with $150,000 of jewelry. "The over-all plan worked to perfection," Sutton later remarked with a certain smugness.[2]   During the months that followed, the daring duo pulled numerous jobs with Sutton gaining entry posing as everything from a policeman to a fireman and a window washer to a carpenter. "We walked in and out of banks as if we owned them. We hit jewelry stores, insurance companies, anything.[3]"

William Francis Sutton was enjoying the notoriety. The news media constantly talked about the notorious actor, the man of many faces, who robbed banks, seemly with impunity. The Banker's Association distributed cautionary bulletins and the police doubled the guards. Victims couldn't identify the thieves, especially Sutton, who thought of himself as a Master of Disguise. At any rate, he kept everybody in a state of confusion, even the police. Not known as a shy man, Sutton seemed to revel in describing his "acting style" in great detail to anyone who would listen.

> "The thing that really had the police so confused was that I was using so many different disguises. I would dye my hair different colors. I had sideburns I could paste on. I had all different types of mustaches . . . If I really wanted to look distinguished I'd wear a Vandyke. I could make my eyebrows very heavy by intertwining separate little patches of hair . . . I had a whole set of hollowed out corks to alter the shape of my nose . . . On the spur of the moment, I'd affect the barest hint of a lisp or accent. . . .[4]"

Willie "The Actor" Sutton, who nobody had yet identified, continued to improvise and enlarge his repertoire and, almost like a little kid, play all the parts. He was enjoying himself immensely and thought of himself as smarter than his victims. For example, in his book, written years later, he describes the only possible weakness of his M.O., his biggest concern:[5]

> ". . . the thing I was most concerned about at the beginning, was that after I had entered the bank and taken everybody under control I was still going to be totally dependent upon the willingness of the manager to open the vault for me. Never once did I have the slightest problem; it always amazed me

how quickly they complied. I'd hold out that psychological bribe to them, letting them believe that if it was their own safety that was involved they'd have held out courageously, and immediately we'd be heading for the vault."

Sutton was quite intelligent and while incarcerated spent a great deal of time studying. He considered himself a competent amateur psychologist, which is apparent from the way he describes his control over the bank managers. He was also a gutsy and very self-assured, egotistical little guy who was always pushing the envelope without regard for the consequence. His targets, mostly banks and big jewelry stores, were often in the busiest parts of the city, with streets full of pedestrians and policemen on constant patrol. There's a story about two heist men of reputation who were recruited by Dutch Schultz, the infamous New York City mobster, who supposedly was Sutton's fence. Schultz, as the story goes, tried to persuade Sutton to put them to work.

He reluctantly agreed and took them downtown to a restaurant right across the street from the target bank and explained the plan to them. The two men took one look at the street teeming with people and the dense traffic and the police cars that passed by at regular intervals and broke into a cold sweat. The next morning the would-be thieves took their concerns and objections to Schultz at his headquarters. As they explained all the reasons why the bank couldn't safely be robbed, Sutton and his partner were actually cleaning out the vault.[6] Such is the stuff that legends are made of.

The obvious risks didn't get Sutton captured for the second time. It was the jealous wife of a philandering husband, who also happened to be his partner. She fingered both Sutton and her husband, Bassett, who spilled his guts big-time, confessing to thirty-seven robberies they had committed and to several they didn't commit–anything to keep the peace. For his part, Sutton confessed to nothing. He hadn't robbed anybody, didn't work with Bassett, didn't know who the fences were. He didn't know anything. Apparently, not many people did. More than a hundred witnesses were brought in to identify Willie Sutton as the thief and their tormentor. Out of all those witnesses, only the porter in the M. Rosenthal heist could identify Sutton with conviction.

Sutton never confessed to anything, but was none-the-less convicted of the Rosenthal robbery and sent to Sing Sing. He had been free for twenty-two months and was now nearly 30 years old. The sentence was 30 years.[7]

Sutton could now be classified as a long-timer. He saw no way he could live through this.[8] First, he owed the state of New York the six and half years left from his previous sentence. Only after serving that sentence would his latest sentence, the 30 years, commence. He might make it, but he'd be an old man. There is a sort of rule in convict experience: When you're looking at that many years, maybe 40 or 50 years or longer in the slammer, one of two things happens: You become resigned to your fate and meld into the prison culture, making the best of the situation. Alternatively, despair and desperation crush your spirit and completely dominate your mind. Then there is only one all encompassing thought. Regardless of the risks and dangers involved, you must escape! Sutton's spirit may not have been crushed, but he sure had escape on his mind.

Sing Sing was different from when he was there five years earlier in 1926. The institution had been completely rebuilt, so much so that it was almost unrecognizable. The new prison was billed by the press as escape proof–you couldn't saw your way out or dig your way out or climb out. In less than two years, Sutton and one other inmate named Johnny Eagen had done just that, they climbed out. Actually, they sawed their way out of their cells, unlocked seven secured doors (Sutton was also a self-proclaimed, premier lock picker) and, with two stolen ladders lashed together, climbed up to an unmanned guard tower and down to the ground on the other side using a rope that was used to hoist supplies from the ground up to the tower during the daylight hours.

Unlike most breakouts, Sutton's was well planned and executed. His wife, Louise, was waiting a short way from the prison in a car with money and clothes for both escapees. With help from friends outside, the two managed to get more cash and hide out in an apartment in a quiet part of Brooklyn.[9]

New York was neither a safe place for Sutton to stay nor to do business any more. After his last arrest and the confession of Basset, the authorities were on to his methods. So, after only a short time while waiting for the heat to cool, Sutton was on his way to Philadelphia to set up shop. But first, he and Johnny Eagan "borrowed" around $30,000 dollars from the Corn Exchange Bank on 10th Street in New York.[10]

In Philadelphia, Sutton lived on Chestnut and Forty-second Street with a girl friend and conducted business in the surrounding communities–Ambler, Doylestown and Allentown. Occasionally there would be a foray into the hinterlands, up around Buffalo, New York or out towards Pittsburgh. Meanwhile, in Philadelphia the banks were taking all necessary precautions required to keep Willie Sutton at bay. Undaunted, Willie and two other men, Eddie Wilson and Joe Perlango, took the Corn Exchange Bank located on 60th Street and Market.

The robbery, which was well planned, went off without a hitch. Two things were memorable about it. One was the haul, they only got about $11,000. That was a major disappointment.

Two, this was Sutton's last robbery in Pennsylvania, let alone Philadelphia. He was captured a short time later, tried and convicted, and the judge threw the book at him–25 to 50 years. And, of course, he also owed all that time in New York state. It was 1934 and Sutton had been free for a little over a year. Now he was on his way to Eastern State Penitentiary.

Chapter 5

Strike Two

Joe Corvi was released from Huntingdon in the spring of 1935 with ten dollars in his pocket and a one-way train ticket to Philadelphia, both compliments of the Commonwealth of Pennsylvania. He had grown a little taller, filled out some, now weighing close to 190 pounds, and, hopefully, had gotten a little smarter. Joe was nineteen years old and had spent 20 months in prison. It was an experience he'd just as soon not repeat. On the other hand, he had no regrets. He'd paid his money and taken his chances.

Aboard the train Joe had a seat to himself next to the window. He could feel the rhythm of the steel wheels hitting the joints in the rails. Through the window he watched the countryside pass: trees and pastures and dusty country roads. Occasionally, the train would pass through a town, its whistle blowing a mournful tune, and he could see ordinary people walking on the streets or in their automobiles–free people. He was free now. The feeling was indescribable.

His parole plan involved living with his father, who still had the place on Rosewood Street. Brother John was still living at home as were two of his three sisters. John had reported finding a job for his brother, working on a laundry truck. Actually, there was no job, but the parole officer, who never investigated, was satisfied that a job was waiting. It was still in the midst of the depression and jobs were difficult to find, especially for an ex-convict. After all, there were hundreds, thousands of law abiding husbands and fathers out there trying to support their families, so who was going to give a job to a thief, rehabilitated or not? Joe found himself doing odd jobs and working as casual labor when he could. Basically, he was working for pocket money. Had he not been living at home, times would have been tough. At nineteen, he wanted more than pocket money and his present situation was both discouraging and frustrating. Besides, all the laying around was boring.

It wasn't long before the old ways beckoned. He returned to the burglary business, only this time decided he'd be more careful, choosing targets more carefully and working more consistently. After all, this was his profession. Potential victims were chosen from the more prosperous neighborhoods in Delaware, Montgomery, and Chester counties–places like the "Mainline" of Philadelphia, where the citizens had never felt the pinch of the recession. There were plenty of opportunities in those neighborhoods of the rich and famous–places populated with large estates and huge stone mansions with driveways that today could double as an airport runway.

Joe executed one burglary each week, but had to spend several days reconnoitering target neighborhoods and planning the jobs. Once again, he was looking for signs of extended absence or consistent patterns of coming and going–situations that would offer him a window of opportunity. Houses with dogs, Joe found, offered the best chances of a successful haul. The owners mistakenly thought the dog would protect the house and it probably would have if it was possible. With Joe, it wasn't possible because he'd trap them in a room. However, he had to experience a sort of epiphany before he learned about managing house dogs.

––––––––––

The room looked empty as Joe peered through the window. It was a big room with a fireplace halfway along the long wall and well furnished with over-stuffed chairs, floral sofas and hardwood tables. In one corner there was a grand piano. Nice room, nice house. He'd jimmied the window handily and crawled inside when he heard the low, menacing growl. Joe stood, facing the danger. He never used a flashlight, because they could be seen from outside the house. However as his eyes adjusted to the dim light, he made out the dark form of a very large and, therefore, scary animal. "Cheez and crackers," was all he had to say.

Of course, there wasn't time for a speech and no time to retreat either, not without leaving "something" behind. He quickly located a door and then facing the animal with his jimmy bar at the ready, carefully scuttled toward the exit. The dog advanced, stiff legged, still snarling, with guard hair erect. Joe was lucky this wasn't an attack dog. He was sweating as he continued inching toward the door, all the while talking sweet nothings to Fido. Finally he reached the door and managed to bolt from the room, getting the door closed just before the dog slammed into it with a fit of furious barking. Shaken, Joe stood with his back against the door for a moment and gathered his wits.

After blocking the door with a table, just in case, Joe carefully scouted out other rooms until he found one with a door that led to the room he had originally entered. The dog was still working on the door Joe had used as an exit, ferociously tearing at the wood and barking. Joe slammed the second door shut and jammed a chair beneath the doorknob for good measure. Then he took a huge gulp of air and grinned to himself. He had that vicious creature penned up! Then, as usual, Joe made his way to the master bedroom. The people who lived here, Joe thought as he scanned the room, were careless as hell. They left valuables of all sorts laying around in plain sight. The top of the huge dresser was a regular treasure trove. Then it dawned on him–people don't hide their valuables when they have a watch dog, a habit that makes the job of a thief all the easier. All he had to do was pen up the dog, and the house, as well as its contents, were all his.

Some people kept small fortunes in their houses. On one occasion Joe picked up a beautiful diamond necklace that was just laying on a dressing table, right where the lady of the house had removed it. The piece had strings of huge diamonds, like the ones that might have adorned Cleopatra's royal neck. He sold the piece to a fence for eighteen thousand dollars, one of the biggest hauls he ever made.

A fair number of the homes he visited had small safes or strong boxes. Joe never attempted to open them on the spot.

Rather, he'd simply tumble them down the stairs and carry the box out into the driveway when the job was done. Then he'd retrieve his car, which was always parked a block or two away, drive back, pick up the safe and leave. When he got to a safe place, he'd apply a sledge hammer to the dial mechanism and beat it into submission or simply chisel off one side. He'd locate the seam where the side and top were attached and use a cold chisel and a three pound hammer. In most cases the side would peel off revealing the contents.

Sometimes the contents of the safe would be nothing more than divorce papers, birth certificates, and an array of other useless stuff. Other times he would find what a thief is supposed to find in a safe—money and jewelry and bonds. In one home, he really hit the jackpot. By the time he finished scooping everything out of the safe, Joe had a pile of very expensive jewelry and a bonus in the form of ten, one thousand dollar bills. It was tough to convert large denomination currency like that, but Joe had a friend, named Weasel, who worked in a bank. For a small fee Weasel would trade the large bills for something more spendable.

Joe Corvi was doing quite well with his business. He only worked three or four days a week, counting reconnaissance, planning, and loot disposal time. He had plenty of money, but was careful about his spending. For example, rather than drive a new automobile, he drove a two-year old Buick. He dressed well, but not ostentatiously. He was generous, but not too generous. On the other hand, he made some strategic and tactical errors. He had been working the same exclusive territory for two years. He always entered the same way, with minimal damage, tried to avoid causing unnecessary damage or disorder inside the house, although this was difficult whilst tumbling safes down flights of stairs. Mostly, he took only cash and jewelry, never bulky stuff, regardless of the value, and never messed with a safe unless he could easily move it off the premises. And, of course, he favored houses with guard dogs.

Joe had been too busy, in the same territory, for too long. The local police began staking out his favored neighborhoods and became more alert to foreign cars and suspicious people roaming the streets late at night. Finally, one night the police followed Joe right to his target, let him burglarize it, and captured him as he walked out the back door with loot on his person. He had long since resigned himself to getting caught. As the old thief said, "If you're going to play the game, sooner or later you'll have to pay the piper." He surrendered to the officers without a word of protest.

The last job, the one where he was captured, was in Merion Township. The police detectives interrogated him for several days, searched everywhere and found virtually nothing to link him to other jobs. Finally Joe admitted to one other burglary, besides the one he'd been caught on, just to make the police quit looking. He pled guilty based on the logic that if you're guilty, plead innocent, and lose the gamble, the judge is going to be more severe in doling out punishment. He was convicted and sentenced to five to twenty years. He'd shot a crap!

What really irked him was when the Captain of Detectives at Merion Township said, "Did ya know that the people you stole from made more money than you did on the burglary? Everyone of them probably inflated their insurance claims by double the amount you took from them. Ya actually did 'em a favor." Then he laughed. Joe thought about that for a moment and laughed quietly. *Hell, fair is fair. We're all thieves at heart.*

Corvi was sent to Eastern State Penitentiary, the reception center for the eastern part of the state, and placed in quarantine. When he entered Huntingdon the first time, words like formidable and foreboding came to mind. Eastern State was something else again. It looked like a huge medieval fortress with 30-foot high stone walls that were 12-feet thick at the base, parapets and castellated guard towers, and no less than three gates at the main and only entrance. There was a new gateway that was built in 1937-1938. The original, an imposing portcullis, was directly behind the new gate and two more iron gates were behind the original. Only one gate could be opened at a time.[1] Entering this place was like entering another world. In fact, that's exactly what it was–a virtual micro universe, completely self-contained, that existed in the middle of Philadelphia. Within that universe was a unique social, political and administrative structure which was completely isolated from the outside world.

Eastern State Penitentiary or Cherry Hill, as it was sometimes called because the prison was built on the site of a large cherry orchard, was the reception center for the entire eastern part of the state. The name the inmates used was simply The House. Here a new prisoner was put in quarantine, cell block fourteen, until he was classified. Classification was supposed to involve analyzing medical, vocational, and educational history in order to determine which institution would be best for the prisoner.

What actually happened, as Joe came to understand, is you were sent to the prison with the next available cell. After about six weeks Corvi was transferred to Graterford Penitentiary, which is located thirty-five miles north of Philadelphia. Joe arrived at his new home in late 1937. Tenuto didn't appear on the scene for another two and a half years. Most significant for Joe was that in Graterford that he meets James Van Sant, a man who not only becomes a life-long friend, but one who became a primary character as the story moves forward. This meeting, like the reacquaintence with Saint will also have to wait for a few more years. In the meantime, the education of Joseph Corvi begins.

Chapter 6

Locked in Graterford

L ong term or short term or any term, incarceration is not the preferred way to spend time, regardless of the institution. In the first place, prisons are truly confining, to state the obvious. Even one of those modern day country clubs where they stash white-collar thieves, where they have comfortable cells that are more like efficiency apartments, indoor swimming pools, tennis courts and open, airy lounge areas, are confining. But Corvi was heading to a bona fide prison with small, sparsely furnished cells, whitewashed walls, and heavy, barred doors that close with a mechanical snarl. Here, the inmates must stand and be counted six times a day and somebody tells them what to do and when to do it. This is one of those places where 1,000 or 1,500 or more men are crowded into ten or fifteen acres of real estate with a very high wall around it–a place where society puts murderers, bank robbers, dope fiends, rapists and burglars like Joe Corvi.

Joe wasn't new to the drill, he'd spent time at Huntingdon Reformatory. He remembered that first view. It was formidable and oppressive. What he saw at Eastern State Penitentiary, where he was sent for classification after sentencing, was something quite different. Now he would be in with the big boys and that first impression had a certain finality to it.

"I was alone in the back of a sheriff's van," he recalled, "just coming from the court house, which was located in the Philadelphia City Hall. After you're sentenced, there's no bags to pack or anything. Hell, you're not going on a vacation. They cuff you and cart you off to Eastern State. My view of the world during that ride was through a narrow, screened slit, one on either side of the compartment. Through those narrow slits I saw the grim stone walls of the prison, armed, uniformed guards and the iron gates. Damn! Talk about a wake-up call. This was when I really knew I was gonna be caged. That realization washed over me like a tidal wave and penetrated even the tiniest crevices in my brain. "

Once inside the gates, Joe, like all newly arrived inmates, had to be mugged and fingerprinted. The first stop was a sparsely furnished office located just inside the front entrance to the prison. He was sitting in a hard, straight-backed chair, one of six lined up against the wall. Two other men waited with him, elbows resting on knees, staring at the floor. Joe decided they were probably reflecting on their sins and the predicament they were in. That's certainly what he was thinking about. There was a single desk with a brown-suited man sitting behind it. He was facing an older guy with a hard face and salt and pepper gray hair cropped short. A number of filing cabinets backed up to one wall. On another wall was a large, framed photograph of Franklin Delano Roosevelt, the picture of another man who Joe guessed was the governor, and still a third photograph containing the image of a stern-faced fellow wearing a blue uniform and a white shirt with an uncomfortable looking starched collar. Joe later found out this man was the present warden of Eastern State, none other than Warden Herbert E. Smith, also known as Bozo and Hardball to the inmates.

The man with the salt and pepper hair rose and headed for the door clutching a paper in his hand. The man behind the desk, a prisoner clerk, who looked like he'd been around awhile, shuffled some papers for a minute or two and looked up. "Corvi," he said tentatively. Joe stood up, walked to the desk and took the now empty chair.

"Joseph John Corvi?"

"That's me," Joe said with a smile. He was a personable, friendly young man who thought a smile was always preferred to a frown. The clerk was not of like mind, but at least he wasn't frowning. This was his job, better than most, but he'd just as soon be elsewhere.

"Five to twenty for Burglary. Residence 2400 Rosewood Street, Philadelphia." The man read aloud to himself from Corvi's file. Joe sat sideways on the uncomfortable chair, his left arm over the back rest. Every once in a while he'd reverse position in an effort to find a more comfortable position. He didn't.

The clerk looked up. "Education?"

This interview is really mindless, Corvi thought. *The man talks to himself like he's reciting some equally mindless prose and clearly doesn't care a damn about what he's doin.* Joe decided he could play this game as well. He answered, "Yeah."

The clerk looked up quickly. Now he was frowning. "How much education, Corvi?"

"High school."

"Graduated?"

"No."

The older man stared at him. "Look, can we get on with it? Either you answer the questions or you can take it up with my boss. You don't want to do that, I'm sure." He paused, making sure the young man in front of him got the message. "How much education?"

"Junior in high school."

And so the interview went for the better part of 30 minutes. Mother's name, father's name, siblings? Where do they live? How long did you reside at your last address? On and on it went. Finally, the clerk opened a book, his finger scrolling down the page. He wrote something on the form he was filling out and then wrote something on another piece of paper and shoved it across the desk at Corvi. Joe picked it up and read it. It had two numbers on it. One was A784 and the other was 14-26.

Joe looked up inquiringly. The clerk said in a monotone, "First number's your new name, it's the name that identifies you while you're a guest here." A miserly smile briefly crossed his face. "Other one's your cell number. The guard outside will take you there now."

Joe, sensing he was dismissed, got up and started to the door. The clerk's voice stopped him. "Best not ta be smart alecky while you're in here. Some folks don't like it." At that the clerk turned his attention to a new file.

Joe was then escorted down a long corridor into a rotunda area, the control center of the prison. Along the way he passed four cell blocks and could see prisoners milling around in small groups or talking in pairs or just standing there alone looking at nothing. He was accompanied by two guards, one on either side of him, and they moved off to the right, finally arriving at cell block 14–where he would spend the next month or two being classified and awaiting a permanent assignment.

Before he was done on the day he walked to his temporary home in cell block 14, Corvi, number A784, was dressed in shades of brown–brown shirt, brown trousers, brown jacket and brown shoes. Even his underwear was brown–prison made, prison issue. And, he was thinking, *cheez and crackers.*

Prisons are different. It's almost like they each have distinct personalities. You get just a hint of the differences by what the inmates call them. Alcatraz, located in San Francisco Bay, was called The Rock; Leavenworth, the federal prison in Leavenworth, Kansas, is the Hot House; and, Dannemorra is Siberia. Most prisoners would say that all prisons have three things in common: They were built to keep prisoners inside, control them, and intimidate them. Otherwise they're all different and, to the inmates, those differences can be significant.

For Corvi there were only two alternatives, and they were almost dependent upon a whimsy or the toss of a coin. In spite of a lot of talk about rehabilitation, where an inmate wound up depended upon where the first cell became available. He would either stay with the population in Eastern State or would be moved to Graterford, known as The Farm to inmates, north of Philadelphia in Montgomery County where Perkiomen Creek runs under the bridge you have to cross to get to the prison. And there were major differences between the two institutions. And although Corvi wouldn't learn about it for several years, the biggest difference was in the administrative personnel, particularly the guards.

Most of the guards at Eastern were recruited from the Philadelphia metropolitan area. In other words, they were city folk.

Likewise, the inmates were predominately city folk and a large percentage were from Philly and its surrounds. Graterford was, and still is, a rural area and the guards were recruited from that area. To the Graterford guards, these city people they were receiving could just as well have come from another planet–they acted different and they talked different. But the real difference was the guards who came from an entirely different culture and whose training dictated how they treated inmates. This may sound like a lot of conjecture, but regardless, the Eastern guards tended to be friendlier and required less formality. For example, inmates and guards at Eastern could be on a first name basis and you might see an inmate leaning on a desk in the cell block, visiting with a guard. In Graterford you would see no such behavior and all guards were addressed as Mr. or Sir. The Graterford guards seemed to be suspicious, formal and remote. At Eastern, the atmosphere was almost casual. If you were locked in cell block 7 and wanted to see a sick friend in cell block 3, the hospital block, you'd just walk over and see him. At Graterford, while the guards were always addressed respectfully, the inmates seldom enjoyed the same treatment. An inmate was normally addressed as, "Hey You or simply Inmate." Prisoners didn't wander far from the entrance to their cell block without a pass or a uniformed escort. Unless it was time to walk to your assigned work place, a classroom, or the dining room, you stayed close to home. The atmosphere at Graterford was much more strict and tense.

Part of the problem may have been the size of the prisoner population at the two institutions. Graterford had about twice as many prisoners as Eastern.[1] And while the latter   locked 50 or 60 men on a block, Graterford locked 400 men. One result of this difference was that the guards at Eastern had a much higher awareness of personal problems among the inmates. If a man was going through "troubled times" such as the death of a family member or marital problems, a guard would know about it and would tend to overlook minor rule infractions. At Graterford, inmates toed the line regardless. The exception was a death in the family, preferably your own.

Another big difference between the two prisons was that the educational and vocational opportunities were far better at Graterford, especially the educational opportunities. And Joe Corvi, prisoner A784, who was finally assigned to Graterford, took full advantage of what was offered. Joe wasn't in Graterford for very long before he discovered some of these "opportunities." One involved a course in drafting offered through the International Correspondence Schools. The prison provided a classroom and all of the necessary equipment, but used ICS material. Students who had already graduated and had improved their skills doubled as teachers. Joe completed the course and developed skills that would prove useful later on.

Nor was life at Graterford all work and learning. Like many of the inmates, Joe also took advantage of the available sports opportunities. Yard out, the exercise period, was a period of several hours every day that was treasured by all the inmates. It was so treasured that it was something an inmate would be deprived of as punishment for some infraction. Sports made the outside time even better. Graterford's athletic facilities were far superior to those at either Holmesburg or Eastern State. There was a baseball and softball diamond which also doubled as a football field in the late fall and winter. The prison wall on the west side of cellblock A, where the exercise yard was located, accommodated twenty handball courts. Weight lifting areas were also included, some being located in the spaces between the cell blocks. There were also a couple of Bocce courts. Although not an athletic event, the men played dominoes on both wooden and concrete benches located along the edges of the yard. The dots on the dominoes were sometimes colored to transform the little wooden blocks into a pinochle deck.

Gambling, although frowned upon, is common in all prisons. The inmates at Graterford gambled on pinochle and on handball, among other things, with cigarettes being the medium of exchange, since cash is considered contraband in prisons and not allowed inside. The inmates can have money in an account, like a bank account, but it can only be spent in the commissary.

Corvi, being in great physical shape, well coordinated and fast, was quite good at handball. The men usually played doubles and when they couldn't find suitable opponents from the other blocks to compete with, they'd gamble among themselves. At times the outcome of the game was contested.

On one such occasion Corvi and his partner, Johnny Greco, were playing against a team from Germantown, one of whom was a guy named Casey. Casey was a short-armed fellow who also possessed a short temper. He took serious exception to some of Corvi's tactics, which included in-your-face taunting and insulting remarks intended to distract and confuse. One day, Casey' temper flashed and he turned on Joe, throwing roundhouse punches.

"You son-of-a-bitch, I'll teach ya from running off at the damned mouth. Awkward as a damned plow horse am I . . . Shit!" Casey was churning the air with both hands all the time, cursing and calling Joe everything but a human being. Joe, on the other hand, was able to duck, feint or slip Casey's blows easily while delivering jabs and combinations of his own. It wasn't a serious fight, more like a mutual pawing. Nobody got hurt, but Casey was the sort of guy who carried a grudge for a while, not a good thing in a closed community like a prison, where violence of the terminal sort is not at all uncommon.

It turned out that Casey was in the mechanics class at the School House and to get to his classroom area he had to walk through the drafting area where Joe was a student at the time. The tables were arranged on either side of an aisle, and the students sat with their backs to the aisle in order to avoid distractions as other inmates and guards walked about. Given the circumstances, Corvi took the precaution of turning his desk around so he could see who was coming and going. If somebody was going to slip a shiv between his ribs, he wanted to see who it was. After a while Casey cooled off, so nothing ever came of the handball disagreement, but Corvi, just the same, kept his seat facing the aisle.

In addition to the ICS course, Joe also earned a GED during the same period. Subsequently he was drafted by the prison administration to teach other inmates at the elementary level. The director of the school was Dr. Cooper, a soft-spoken, balding, pot-bellied academic, who was, according to Corvi, a prince of a man. Other than Cooper, all staff, teachers and clerks were inmates. Classes were in session during the morning hours. After lunch and one of six daily headcounts, the students would join the rest of the population who were free for yard out. The teachers would normally congregate back at the school house after lunch where they and Dr. Cooper either played word games or just shot the bull.

All vocational and academic activities took place in the School House, which wasn't really a school house at all, but some kind of a warehouse or business place that was inherited by the prison. Vocational training, like drafting and mechanics, was taught downstairs and academics up. The building was present and accounted for long before the prison was built but is no longer, a casualty of the demand for more prison cells and modernization. It was a two storied building, shaped like a large, rectangular salt box and covered with shingles that were bleached grey from years of exposure to the wind and rain and snow and sun. The dimensions were about 90 feet long and 40 feet wide. The first floor had three rooms and the upstairs was one big room compartmentalized by portable black boards. This is where Corvi did his teaching—just readin', 'ritin', and 'rithmetic—for most of the duration of his sentence.

The reading teachers received special training. Here's a sound, here's a word, here's a bunch of words. First, dog, cat, boy and girl. Then short sentences. Then pages. One day the student could read an entire sentence—just like anybody else. Joe described the experience:

"They'd read a lesson or story assigned to them and were, maybe for the first time in their lives, proud of an achievement. These tough, hardened guys, absolutely beamed with pride and pleasure. For some it was a first positive step in the rest of their lives. An incredible experience! Some of these men were fathers in their former lives, who could now go back home and read a story to one of their kids or maybe even help them with their homework."

Joe remembers this experience as one of the most rewarding in his life. Many of the convicts, at that time, were functionally illiterate and that may still be the case. It takes courage for a grown man to admit he can't even read a comic strip or can't write his own name. These people had essentially no skills beyond common labor. It's no wonder they became thieves and robbers and burglars. Some thought the parole board would look more favorably on them if they made the effort to educate themselves. Others simply took advantage of the circumstances and determined to gain from the enforced downtime. But most learned, regardless of the motivation.

"At some point," Corvi explained, "a look of wonderment would light up the face of a killer or a stick up man and it was really a sight to see. All of a sudden, these guys would catch a glimpse of a world they didn't even know existed–the mystical world contained between the covers of a book. In some cases a man would use this new skill to study the law to help get himself from behind the walls. Others knew good and well they were never going to leave prison and used reading as a means of releasing their minds to transport them beyond the walls. "

When Joe became an instructor he was transferred from B-Block to A, where the men involved in maintenance, athletics, kitchen and bake shops, weave shop and teaching were locked. Joe was housed in the gallery section, the second tier of cells, about midway down the first half of the block. A person could stand on the gallery walkway, which was made of reinforced concrete, and look down on the corridor that was about 20 feet wide with cells located on either side. The block is actually about 700 feet long and split in the middle, with a walkway between the two sides. This walkway is where the block guard station is located–and the controls that open and close the cells. The door mechanism is mechanical. A guard pulls one of eight levers and 50 doors slide open or close simultaneously. If a prisoner is being locked down as punishment, an additional lock, one that is incorporated on each individual door, can be operated with a key,. Each section formed by the division of the split mentioned above houses at least 200 inmates, more with double occupancy. There are 50 cells in both the upper and lower tiers on each side. This corridor is actually called the cell block. Down the middle of the cell block, spaced about 20 feet apart, are radiators with the steam supplied by the prison powerhouse.   The radiators, with a board or piece of plywood laid across them, converted to tables where inmates could congregate and, perhaps, play dominoes or pinochle on those days when the weather wouldn't permit yard out.   There are five cell blocks, all around 700 feet long and all on the north side of a quarter mile long central, or main corridor. Laundry, maintenance, weave shop, tailor shop, shoe shop and the school building are all on the south side. Inmates walked from their cell blocks up or down the main corridor to work.

For meals, the inmates filed, in two rows, down the length of the cell block and into the block dining room–all, that is, except A-Block which had no dining room of its own. The men from this block shared a dining room with those locked in B-Block, which was the reception block where new boarders were temporarily stored awaiting work assignments. The food was brought in from the kitchen along a corridor located at the extreme end of the cell blocks and placed on steam table for serving.   The dining areas were built to accommodate approximately 400 inmates at a time. While dining, the men sat on wooden benches in front of a narrow table that seated seven men.   Interestingly, while eating, each inmate faced the back of the man in front of him. And there was no talking–just eat and leave.

The room that would have been a dining room for A-Block was converted into a motion picture theater.   Aside from the entertainment function, movie time was also time for retribution. Many a time a movie would come to an abrupt end when a man ran screaming out of the room with blood spurting out of one or more shiv holes. The lights would come on and there would be a search as the inmates vacated the theater. Often there might be as many as 15 or 20 shivs left scattered on the floor.

At Graterford there were five cell blocks, A - E, laid out parallel to each other with a 25-foot open area between them. This area, as well as the main exercise yard, could be used for exercise, although the main yard was located west of A-Block. As a matter of fact, the handball courts were spaced along the outside perimeter wall of the prison and were flanked by two guard towers.

There were 400 cells on each cell block and, at the time, one man was locked per cell. Each cell was six feet wide, 12.8 feet deep and a little over eight feet high. The standard equipment was found in each cell–a steel bunk, a stool, a small chest for gear, a desk-like work area and, of course, the ever present hopper and small sink. The steam radiators were located on the wall above the sink. There was one outside window in each cell. This small space was the home of at least one man and sometimes, with a full house, two men. Regardless. It was the only space a man could call his own and that small bit of privacy, such as it was, was sacred. When an inmate walked down the gallery of the second tier or down the main corridor of the first tier, he never looked directly into a person's cell, except maybe to say hello to a friend. Joe, from past experience, knew better. A newcomer might make the mistake, but only once. An unwanted glance into an occupied cell would be met with an angry response like, "What the fuck are you looking at?" Everybody learned, one way or another, to respect the privacy of others.

Of course, the guards could and did look into any cell they wanted to at any time. At night it happened every 30 minutes. A flashlight lit up the cell to make sure the inmates were all present and accounted for. On occasion this inspection routine was worth a little humor at the expense of the guard. This might come under the heading of cruelty to guards–one of the few times an inmate could get by with it.

Lights out was at nine o'clock and that meant the cells were thrown into complete darkness. If a new guard was on duty, when he came along doing his periodic headcount checks, he'd look in each cell with a flashlight. The inmates that were still awake for some reason could always hear the guard coming long before he arrived at their cell door. When the guard approached his cell, the inmate would either sit on his stool or lie in bed, in the dark mind you, holding a book in his hands as if reading. The guard invariably would flash the light in and walk a step or two before the scene registered. Then he'd do a double take, return and ask the inmate what he was doing. The inmate would look up innocently and reply, "Why, uh, I'm reading a book. Nothing wrong with that is there?" The guard would walk away just shaking his head. Can you imagine what kind of story he'd tell the next guard he saw? "D'ya know what I saw one of these dummies doin' . . . ?" It must have been good for a laugh at the expense of the new guy on the block.

No prison is without its own segregation or solitary unit and even there some humor is found. At Graterford the segregation unit was called the Klondike, probably because it was isolated from the prison itself, being located between the prison and the south wall toward the eastern end of the property. Secondly, it was relatively cold in the winter and steamy hot in the summer. The building, which has since been replaced, was L-shaped, single-storied and constructed of brick. Twenty-four cells, measuring 6-feet by 9-feet, were arranged, sixteen in the long leg of the 'L' and eight in the shorter leg. Each cell faced an eight-foot aisle way and the only windows were along the wall opposite the cells.

The entire front of the cell is iron bars with a 30-inch door on the left-hand side, sort of like an animal cage at the zoo. The only furnishings are the iron cot welded to the wall, the hopper located in the front of the cell next to the door, and a small basin in the same corner but mounted above the hopper. The mattresses are stored in the aisle way, outside the cells during the day and are issued to the inmates after the evening meals. The only clothes were those an inmate had on his back. Once a week there was a shower and each man got a half hour per day exercise period, one man at a time. The rest of the time you spent either sitting on the hopper or the floor. The cot had a steel, lattice work on which you put the mattress, when you got it. It wasn't the most comfortable arrangement for sitting.

Each cell had a vent to the outside on the wall in the back of the cell, but this did little to clean the room of stale body odor and putrid fumes emanating from the hopper, which lacked the goose-neck containing water to prevent sewage odors from backing up into the cell. The vent, which really didn't ventilate anything, did have some utility value. The inmates used the vent ducts to communicate back and forth with the cells on the extreme ends of the unit. Since the front of the cell was simply open bars, close neighbors could easily be communicated with. Of course, it was like a party line; everyone could listen in.

Those inmates in segregation for the first time would first hear the faint sound of voices, but didn't understand how the system worked and would ask a neighbor where the voices were coming from. Corvi remembers this story:

"One young man, a first time 'guest' in the unit," Joe related, "asked his next door neighbor about the voices he was hearing. He was told to shout really loud down into the hopper and the person he wanted to talk with would respond."

This explanation, as the story goes, was followed by a brief silence while the newcomer got himself positioned with his head over the cast iron throne. Then the shouting commenced, a bit half-heartedly at first. This was understandable, given the awful stench that was wafting up from the sewer. Of course, there was no response. When he complained that he couldn't be heard, the neighbor told him, "Ya gotta really stick yer head way down inta da hopper." The young man did as he was told, apparently anxious for some conversation. The next sounds were those of a fierce gagging spasm. The stink coming out of that hopper was foul, really foul, maybe like the stink of an outhouse on a really hot summer day, if you can imagine sticking your head right into the glory hole. That gagging soon turned into violent retching and then it sounded a lot like a first class hurling exhibition. Pretty soon a weak voice could be heard saying "Fuck this! I didn't wanna talk to the bastard anyhow."

———————

In prison, most of the men mind their own business and get along. They learn, they work, and they play. It's not much different than outside except it's a closed society and the citizens are convicted criminals. A lot of books about prison life tell of fear and anger and violence. And, of course, there's a fair amount of all three, but there are a lot more guys who screwed up and just want to do their time and get out than there are of the violent sort. These guys work and play and see some humor in their situation. They survive. The trouble is, the violent ones and the trouble makers are the ones that get the press. Gary Henman, a former warden at Marion Penitentiary in Illinois, explained. "Most inmates come into prison, follow the rules, do their time, get something out of it, and never come back. But some come in and actually form their own prison culture. These men refuse to conform or follow any rules. They want to conduct business in here just like when they are on the streets. They want to steal, sell drugs, whatever, and they are very disruptive.[2]" There are people like this in any society and there always have been.

Chapter 7

Scaling the Wall

Botchie and Freddie 'Saint' Tenuto originally met at Holmesburg County Prison where Botchie was serving time for robbery and Saint was awaiting trial for homicide. Following his trial, Saint was convicted and sentenced to 20 to 40 years. He was sent to Eastern State Penitentiary for classification and subsequently sent to Graterford. Botchie, after finding out about his detainer from New York, escaped from Holmesburg, was captured, and within a short time found himself at Eastern State where he had, by his own reckoning, at least 32 years to serve.

When Saint arrived at Graterford, Joe Corvi had already served over two of his five to twenty-year sentence for burglary. Joe could stand on the gallery outside his cell in A-Block and look down to Saint's cell. They remembered each other from the days at Huntingdon and although the short and swarthy Saint was cordial enough, he hadn't changed much. He still distanced himself from the other men, always minding his own business. He and Joe would exchange greetings once in a while and, on occasion would meet during yard out and, perhaps, play a little handball together. However, the relationship remained distant.

Even though Joe saw Saint often since they locked in the same cell block, Saint wasted no time drawing a line in the sand. It was like a sign that said, "Don't mess on me." He had nothing against Joe Corvi, treating everyone the same way. He quickly demonstrated that although a little older and now a welterweight, he was still deadly with his hands. There wasn't a boxing ring at Graterford, but there was at Eastern. The inmates prevailed upon Eastern's Warden Smith to allow 'his guys' to fight against local professionals. A local Philadelphia fight manager and bookmaker, Blinkey Palermo, brought some of his fighters fairly regularly.

Blinkey had one fellow in his stable who was supposed to be really good, maybe even a title contender, whose name was Billy Fox. Billy got matched with Saint, who was temporarily transferred to the House for the fight. The little Italian still stalked his opponents like a mongoose goes after a cobra, had extremely quick hands and, if anything, was a stronger fighter and more powerful puncher than he was a few years earlier. It's unlikely that Blinkey had in mind getting his prize contender unraveled by a convict who was giving away 40 pounds. But that's exactly what happened. Saint calmly and methodically delivered swarms of jabs and combinations punctuated with thundering power punches–hooks and uppercuts. Fox wasn't a bad fighter, he just couldn't handle the Saint.

———————

At some point Saint took sick and got a medical transfer over to Eastern. Or may he was faking, as future events might suggest. After a while Joe noticed that he was missing and heard that Saint was on 3 Block at Eastern State, the hospital psycho ward and geriatric center. Of course, Botchie was already housed at Eastern. The two men soon became reunited. It happened during a yard out and Botchie was clearly surprised to see Tenuto, who was supposed to be elsewhere. Tenuto, on the other hand, had been looking for his old prison mate. After a brief time getting reacquainted Saint asked Botchie about his escape from Holmesburg.

"Jeez, all a sudden you were gone," Saint said. "I heard you sort a hitched a ride out the front gate." He laughed. Had Botchie not been such a friendly sort, or perhaps because they were former prison mates, the inquiry would have been totally inappropriate. You don't ask personal questions inside. In fact, you don't ask anything at all. At best you'll be told to mind your own business. At worst somebody will get the impression you're a snitch or something. That can be hazardous to your health. However,

Botchie thought nothing of it. Probably thought Tenuto was just happy to see a familiar face.

"Yeah, it worked slick as hell 'til that liquor store clerk showed up," Botchie replied. "Shot the son-of-a-bitch."

"Heard about that. Tough luck."

The two men walked in silence for a bit, having a smoke and enjoying the outside. Saint looked at Botchie, a little hesitantly, and then asked a crucial question. "You still interested in getting outa here?"

Botchie's head snapped up. After a moment he said, "It's all I think about. Hell, I'm damned near 40 years old and still lookin' at 30 years ya know. What'd you be thinking about?"

"Figured. Me too." Saint's black eyes glittered and looked a little distant. If you looked into them, you'd see he was already on the other side of the walls. "Look," he continued, "I figure we could put an escape plan together over at Graterford. You're the only guy I know got the guts for this. Already done it." He paused. "Think you can get a transfer?"

"I can try."

Saint returned to Graterford a short time later. Botchie requested and was given a hearing with the Eastern State Staff Board. He asked for a transfer and provided a simple explanation. "If I ever get out a here again," he stopped and looked at the board members a little sheepishly and continued. "Legally, I mean . . . I got to have some sort of trade so I kin make a livin'. Otherwise I'll be right back in again." He stopped talking for a moment, hoping he'd smoothed out that little misstatement. "Graterford's got the trades and the industry. I could learn how ta make a living and be worth a damn. Hell, right now I don't know nothing but, ah," he paused, thinking, "but what I do," he finished with a nervous grin. After a short but anxious wait Botchie learned that his request had been granted and he was going to be transferred.

Tenuto, back home on cell block A, had been busy. He intended to do this with or without a partner. First he reconnoitered the various shops, finding out what equipment was available, how free the inmate workers were to move about, and how fussy the supervision was. He focused on the maintenance shops and finally decided on the Glazier's Shop for himself.

When Botchie arrived at Graterford he was initially assigned to the tailor shop, which was fine since there was no plan as yet. He and Tenuto got together–not so often as to make it obvious–and talked about where Botchie should try to get assigned. They decided the electric shop would be best because of the availability of certain critical material such as heavy conduit, wire and tools. Failing in that, any job in the maintenance shop would do and then a transfer might be possible.

C. J. Burke was the Deputy Warden at Graterford–the guy you had to see to get a job transfer among other things. He was a 25-year veteran of the Pennsylvania prison system and carried his tall, lean frame ramrod straight as you might expect from State Policeman. And, although a gruff, plain-spoken man, he had a reputation as a fair man. If you were straight with him, he'd be straight with you. If not, there were consequences.

His office, really a suite of offices, was toward the end of the main corridor between cell blocks D and E. An inmate doesn't just walk into the D. S.'s office and ask for a few minutes of his time. There's a procedure. Any inmate desiring an interview writes the request and gives it to his Block Sergeant. In Botchie's case this was Sergeant Bill Myers, who worked on the day shift. Myers relayed the request to one of the clerks in Burke's office. Sure enough, on the morning following the submission of his request, he was told to report to the D. S.'s office. This announcement was made by way of the standard prison intercom system–the guard hollering from the guard station "Van Sant, report to the Deputy Warden's office."

Botchie did as he was told, waiting in the outer office until he was told by an inmate clerk that it was his turn. He entered the D.S.'s office and approached his desk before speaking. Burke had Botchie's request for an interview on his desk in front of him. Without looking up Burke said, "What can I do for you Van Sant?"

"Well, Sir, Major Burke, I'd like a job transfer. It ain't that I don't like the tailor shop or nothing like that. Don't mind it at all. But I don't think I'd like being a tailor when I get released.

I've always found electrical stuff interesting and have heard it's a good trade. Anyhow, Sir, I'd like to get transferred to the electrical shop."

There was a moment of contemplative silence after Botchie delivered his pitch. Although the silence was brief, the vacuum created forced Botchie to keep talking. "I know I've not been a model prisoner and that, but I think if I could get into the electrical shop it would sure help me mend my ways. . . ."

Botchie forced himself to stop his nervous chatter, fidgeted around, and finally settled down to await an answer. It was short. "Okay. I'll see to the paper work."

Botchie had expected approval, but was none-the-less surprised, and for reasons only he knew, pleased. "Thank you, Major Burke, 'preciate it." A vague excitement filled him as he left the office.

Now that Botchie was assigned to maintenance he was moved from E-Block, where people who worked in the Welfare Shops, like the tailor shop and shoe shop, locked and into A- Block, the block Tenuto called home. Despite being neighbors, the two men spent little time together and most of that time was during yard out. Nor did anyone else appear to take any special note of the newcomer. Oh, the inmates knew he was there alright, but there was no such thing as a "Welcome Wagon" to greet newcomers on the block and give them goodies. In the house, friendships did develop occasionally, but when they did it was almost by accident–a word of greeting, a chance meeting or perhaps a close working proximity. Sometimes it was simply an event that begged a question from the curious.

———

For the evening meal, in fact all meals, the cell blocks were disgorged of inmates one level at a time. First, what's called the block, the first floor, is emptied. Two rows of prisoners on A-Block walk out through the rear of the block and turn right on the kitchen corridor heading to the B-Block dining room. They enter the dining room in two rows, walking to the dual steam table setup at the front end of the room. Once there, the men turn left or right, pick up a tray and are served their food. When the block cells are empty, a guard opens the gallery cells and these men repeat the process.

Joe Corvi, who locked in the gallery, followed the same route to the dining room, walking in the right-hand lane. As he slowly made his way down the food service line, he extended his tray. A large, bald, black, inmate named Curley slopped some potatoes on Joe's tray. Half the food fell back into the pot.

Meals are kind of an important event for most men in prison. It's not a social thing at all, but was important none-the-less, if for no other reasons than to satisfy hunger and maintain a routine. Portion sizes are important too and strictly enforced by the guards. When Joe motioned with his tray that Curley should replace the potatoes that fell back into the pot, the attendant looked around quickly, and seeing that the guard was watching, shook his head negatively. Joe repeated the motion and the response was a shrug of the shoulders. Sergeant Schroeder, who was watching this scene, waved at Joe to move on. He didn't. Instead he kept motioning with his tray and insisting, now verbally as well, that Curley replace the lost portion. Small things sometimes get blown out of all proportion. Joe wasn't going to starve to death. It was the principle of the thing.

The Sergeant grabbed Joe by the arm and tried to pull him away from the steam table, attempting to forcibly move him on. This was more than a cheez and crackers affair to Joe. He got really pissed and the guard became more insistent. Joe flung his tray and its contents against the wall in back of the steam table. The half portion of mashed potatoes oozed down the wall before falling to the floor. Now, what should have been an insignificant event was in danger of turning into a riot. Everyone in the dining room was aware of the scene unfolding up front. Everyone tensed for the riotous dance to begin. Amazingly, nothing happened. Joe quietly followed in the line, the Sergeant yabbering at him the whole way, and took a seat at his table–fourth from the back, third seat. There he sat, hands clasped together, staring at the table.

What Joe did was considered a serious misconduct. The last thing needed in a prison is a riot over anything, let alone half a scoop of potatoes. Immediately after supper Sergeant Schroeder came to Joe's cell, ironically number thirteen, and escorted him to the Captain's office for a hearing. There, by some combination of mental agility and verbal prestidigitation, Joe somehow avoided spending 30 days in Klondike–or any other form of punishment for that matter. He was marched back to his cell right under the watchful eyes of nearly two hundred inmates. Those that didn't actually observe this miraculous event soon heard about it via the grapevine.

The very next day, during yard out, numerous curious inmates broke one of the major rules of prison etiquette and asked, however obliquely, what had happened. Others simply grinned and made some inane comment like "Good Show." And indeed it was. One of those making an observation was James Van Sant, who had a reputation for possessing a keen sense of humor. "Well, Pal," he remarked, "Kinda lost your supper yesterday, didn' cha? Hope you're feelin' better." The scene really looked sort of queer. Here's this little guy (Botchie was a little over 5' 7" with shoes on) with a twinkle in his gray eyes, grinning up at Joe Corvi who was over six feet tall. Joe grinned a little sheepishly, "Yeah, well. I'm feelin' okay, thanks."

The little guy thrust out his right hand, "James Van Sant, most folks call me Botchie." He hesitated a moment, still grinning, "I screw things up a lot, ya know."

"Yeah, I heard. You moved into A-Block a while ago. I lock up on the gallery."

Botchie gave Corvi a conspiratorial look, his eyes darting around as if someone might be listening in. "How'd ya do that? Anybody else'd be gettin' sunshine pumped to 'em."

Joe, who was as much a talker as Botchie was a comic, warmed to his subject. "Why I just played like I was deaf. Told them something was wrong with me and I couldn't hear a thing. Asked if I was in trouble or something. Acted innocent. You know."

Botchie looked at him in disbelief. "Just told 'em you're deaf. Right."

"No kidding. Captain Brownlee and the Sergeant were hollering their heads off trying to make me hear. They thought I was sick." Corvi stopped to let that sink in and continued, apparently hoping that the last of the story would make the first of it more believable. "Brownlee even made Schroeder take me back to the kitchen and see that I was fed."

The look of disbelief on Botchie's face dissolved into laughter. Finally, he just walked away shaking his head. "See ya round," he said over his shoulder.

———————

Botchie and Saint were both looking for resources, the stuff required to get out. It didn't take long to decide that the escape would be over the walls, and they were formidable–30 feet straight up. But the wall wasn't the only problem. Whatever equipment was necessary had to be collected and stored and there was the little matter of getting out of their cells and across 100 yards of exercise yard undetected.

The electrical shop had a good supply of one-inch conduit, nipples and L-joints. The trick was to steal the amount of conduit and other material needed without the shortage being noticed. That meant a little bit at a time. One sticky problem was storage. The conduit came in eight foot lengths, but that could be reduced in size easily enough. The men thought about stashing the material right in the shop, but that alternative was risky. Somebody might find the stuff and wonder what was going on. Besides, when the time came, there would be no time to go to the shop, gather material, and then pack it all out to the wall. There were two possibilities right in the cells, the mattresses and the locker boxes that each inmate was allowed to keep in his cell for the storage of personal belongings. The boxes were two feet by four and a half–the right length for half a section of conduit. During routine searches the guards regularly tossed the mattresses looking for contraband–cash, extra packs of cigarettes, drugs. That left the box, but that also posed a couple of potential problems. The guards sometimes searched the boxes which meant a false bottom would have to be built. Second, if a guard tried to push the box around, the extra weight would be noticeable. Some casters were filched from the shop and one was attached to each corner of the box, which now scooted around with ease! That left the little matter of the false bottom.

Inmates don't just start carrying boards through the institution, right under the noses of the guards, and into their cells. But how about if the boards for the bottom were hidden in plain sight? Botchie asked one of the carpenters in the shop to build a tool box for him. Its dimensions were such that the new box could carry, flat, boards that would exactly fit inside his locker box. The carpenter, of course, thought nothing of the request and soon Botchie was carrying his brand-new box all over the prison, including in and out of A-Block. At times he even took it into his cell with him. The guards didn't think anything of it. After all, wasn't he an electrician and weren't those his tools? So what if he also hauled a few pieces of wood as well. Not only did Botchie have a false bottom for his locker box, but he also could carry the pilfered conduit to his cell without attracting attention. The men now had the means of scaling a 30-foot wall. But they still had to figure out how to get out of their cells and, if they managed that, where in the world they would find a place to get over the wall unobserved.

———

Botchie was among a group of kibitzers watching a pinochle game when he discovered Saint standing beside him. He made a barely perceptible motion with his head and, after a moment, walked off. Botchie caught up with him after a while and the two men walked together.

"Ya know," Saint began, "I spend a lot a time at night just looking out the damned window at that wall tryin' to figure how in the world we're gonna even get close to it, let alone climb over. Saint stopped and looked at the wall. It was about 300 feet from A-Block and there were two guard towers, one at either end of the exercise area. One of the towers was right next to the building that housed a visitors area on the first floor and prison administration on the second. He continued. "Ya know how the guards lower that rope to hoist their lunches up to the tower?" He glanced at Botchie, who merely nodded, not understanding where the conversation was heading.

"Yep, one lunch at noon and another at seven o'clock in the evening. Except, ya know, I noticed a funny thing." He paused.

Botchie looked at him. Now he suspected this talk was indeed going somewhere and was getting a little impatient. "You gonna take the rest of the day to get ta the point or somethin'?

Tenuto flashed a rare grin. He was a pretty sober guy most of the time. "Keep yer shirt on. I'll get to it." He paused again, savoring the moment, because he really had something special to share with his friend. "I noticed a thing. The guard in that tower next to administration ain't." He turned to Botchie and actually smiled.

"Ain't? Ain't what?" Botchie was really getting exasperated.

"He ain't in the tower, that's what. There's no guard in the tower on the night shift. Heard they're havin' a problem gettin' people ta work in here. Better wages in the war plants, ya know. I've been watchin' for a couple of weeks just ta make sure. There're no meals being delivered to that guard tower at night."

Now it was Botchie's turn to grin. He finally realized that they knew exactly where they were going over the wall. And those towers were 300 or 400 hundred feet apart. On a stormy night the one guard left wouldn't be able to see them even if he knew they were there. "Now that is news!" he exclaimed.

"Thought you'd like it."

The solution to the problem of exiting the cells was similarly serendipitous. Months had gone by, but only a few weeks since the revelation of the guards. It was a Sunday during yard out, a bright, shiny day. Great for baseball. A bunch of the guys were on the east side of the exercise field playing dominoes or pinochle, whatever. Botchie and a number of others were hiking around the perimeter road, the outer edge of the handball courts actually, and around the ball field close to A-Block. Botchie heard the crack of the bat solidly strike the ball and immediately heard someone holler "heads up." He turned to look just in time to see the baseball arc upwards and outward across right field, smack into the side of A-Block and bounce off onto the ground below. As he stared at what he'd seen, a revelation hit him! Surely at some time windows had been broken by a ball and broken windows need fixing.

Botchie told Tenuto, the glazier, and he told his boss, the maintenance officer, but not before insuring that at least one pane was broken in each of their cells. The maintenance officer sent Tenuto to check the cell block windows and he, of course, found several that were cracked and in need of repair. The window frames were made of steel straps that were spaced in sections in order to accommodate rows of five panes of tempered glass, each 4-inches by 8-inches in size. At the top and bottom of the windows there was a panel of glass, the same size as the others, but these two panels flipped inward in order to allow a flow of fresh air. The hole created by the ventilation panels was covered with a mesh screen reinforced by three steel straps. The entire structure was welded together, and the resulting framework was bolted securely to the window casing.

Saint cut a half dozen panes of glass in advance. On the day the repairs were to begin Botchie happened to be free and Tenuto asked if he could help with the work. No problem. The tower officers were notified that two inmates would be working outside of A-Block. Inmates had to have a guard present while working in a prohibited area. But since the side of the block on which the men would be working was in clear view of the wall, the tower guards could observe them.

Each broken pane was removed and the old putty scraped off the sash. Finally, the new panel was inserted and fresh putty applied. All the while that Tenuto was replacing the glass panes on their own windows, Botchie was carefully loosening the bolts. When the day of escape arrived, they'd simply cut the screen, unscrew the bolts and hide the screens under the bunk.

———————

Almost everything was in readiness for the escape. All that remained was smuggling the conduit into Botchie's cell and requisitioning some extra blankets to prepare dummies for the guards to see when they escaped. After lights out, which was at 9:00 P. M., the guards made a bed check every 30 minutes. They'd walk by the cells and look into each one, using a flash light, just to make certain that nobody had wandered off. Of course, that had never happened. In the ten or twelve years since the prison opened for business, there had never been a break out at Graterford.

Getting the dummies together was pretty simple. The pilfered blankets would provide a human shape and some oakum, the tarred hemp used to pack cast iron soil pipes, would pass for hair from a distance. Moving 20 sections of pipe wasn't particularly difficult either, since the guards were accustomed to seeing Botchie walking around with his tool kit. Every time he had to do some work in the kitchen the most direct route was from the shop area, across the main corridor and down through A-Block to the kitchen corridor. At every opportunity he would stash one or two sections of conduit beneath the false bottom of his foot locker.

Soon everything was ready. Botchie told his accomplice when all the material was assembled and stored in his cell. They agreed that they would leave on the following Sunday at 9:00 P. M. when Walter Winchell's radio broadcast began. Immediately after dinner Botchie would begin to assemble the sections of pipe and hide them under his cot. The only catch would be if there was guard in Tower 2 that night. They'd watch the feeding routine to be sure that no lunch box was delivered. If not, Tenuto would meet his partner right outside of his window. Botchie would hand out the pipe sections and off they'd go.

It was a tough week. The two men, by agreement, avoided each other all week long. Both were anxious, but at the same time extremely excited. After nearly a hr of preparation, everything was a go. Freedom now seemed to be a real possibility. They could taste it, visualize it. They were going to make it!

"Good evening Mr. and Mrs. North America and all the ships at sea–let's go to press," intoned Walter Winchell at precisely 9:00 P. M., September 26, 1941.

Both men immediately snipped the wire on their window and backed out the bolts. The window section was stashed under the bed. Saint appeared beneath Botchie's window in a matter of minutes and started taking the conduit sections handed to him and placing them on the ground. Botchie took a last look around to make sure the dummy looked okay and slipped out the window himself. After a brief discussion the men decided to walk down the right field base line to the wall. That way they would be in the shadow of the hospital and the administration building and less apt to be seen. No problem.

At the base of the wall the men hunched over and began assembling the conduit. First they worked on the section that would form the hook that secured the scaling pipe to the wall. The apparatus was then assembled one section at a time as they pushed the completed sections up the wall. When the hook finally reached the top, they could barely see it. It was turned 90 degrees across the wall and pulled snug to secure it. The two men looked at each other, almost giddy with excitement.

Botchie started up first, but his hands were sweating and slipped on the pipe. He slid back down the pipe and took off his shoes and socks. The shoes were replaced and the socks were used as gloves. This time it worked and he shinnied right up to the top with no trouble. When he got to the top, he threw an arm and leg over the wall and pulled himself up until he sat astraddle it. Saint followed quickly until the men were facing each other, both grinning broadly. So far so good, not a hitch–no glaring lights and no alarm and no shouting.

Now the men were in a hurry. They were exposed on top of the wall and silhouetted to some degree. Saint swung the scaling pipe like a pendulum, back and forth, attempting to gain the elevation needed to swing the 30-foot length over the top of the wall. The pipe broke in two. Saint cursed and the two men stared at each other in dismay. It was Botchie who took action. "Ta hell with this," he exclaimed, "I ain't gonna sit here and wait for those damned screws to come an get me." He swung what was left of the pipe, maybe ten feet, over the top and set the hook. Then he got on his stomach and lowered himself until he could grasp the pipe. He went down the pipe hand under hand until he was hanging at arms length. He took a deep breath and let go, falling into the darkness.

When Botchie landed, Saint could hear a groan of pain followed by some cursing. In a second or two Botchie said, as quietly as possible, "Watch yourself, there's a ledge or curb down here. Try to swing out a little."

Saint tried, but it didn't work. He severely wrenched his back attempting a soft landing. They sat there catching their breath, hearts beating like trip hammers. Botchie felt of his right foot gingerly. "I think it's broke," he muttered. "Damned graceful pair ain't we?"

Saint managed to get himself upright and stood a second gritting his teeth in pain. Then he got hold of his friend and managed to get him upright as well. The two men hobbled off–the halt and the lame–arm in arm toward Skippack Road. After going a short distance, Botchie, who was in considerable pain, told Saint to go on without him, but Saint would have nothing to do with that idea. "We got outa there together, now we're goin' get away together," he said.

By the time they reached the road it was apparent that Botchie couldn't continue. Saint hid him in some dense brush. "I'll go steal a car and come back for you," he said confidently, "I'll bust one headlight so you'll know it's me."

———

Back at Graterford, which wasn't all that far away from where Botchie lay hiding, the escape went undetected. The men went to breakfast and returned to their cells and a count was taken. The two sleeping inmates were not disturbed. The work lines were called at 8:00 and at 8:30 those who didn't have to work were released into the exercise yard. Joe Corvi was among those let out. Joe and some friends headed for the handball courts which were along the wall. There, on court number five, were the remains of the broken conduit. Ignoring the pipe, the inmates continued on to the next court and began to play. They all saw the pipe laying there and probably figured out what was going on, but nobody said a word.

After a while the guards in the yard noticed the pipe as well and hollered up to the tower guards to call the Captain. Everything came to a halt–the work and the play–and all of the inmates returned to their cells for a head count. Two guards walked down the length of the cell block counting noses and then repeated the procedure in the tiers. This procedure took place in all five cell blocks. With the head count completed, the guards carried the tally sheets to the Deputy Warden's office and all the sheets were tallied. No inmates were found to be missing.

Corvi watched in amusement as the search for missing inmates was repeated three times. On the third count, the inmates were ordered to stand at their cell door to be counted. Sergeant Kocher found those two inmates still 'sleeping' in their bunks. The State Police was notified and immediately dispatched officers to form a search party. From that day forward all inmates had to stand at their cell door to be counted.

———

Botchie, who was well off the penitentiary grounds, lay in the bushes all day. Evening fell and it grew dark, still no Saint. He began to suspect his friend had been captured and decided to try making his own way. The going across the uneven terrain was painful so he decided to use the road. When a vehicle with two headlights approached he ducked back into field, taking whatever cover was available. But when the next car came by, there was no cover. He tried to make himself look like the ground. The car was being driven by a State Trooper returning home from the search.

The trooper, gun drawn, cocked, and aimed, asked Botchie where he thought he was going. Botchie kept his sense of humor despite his predicament. "There's no question where I'm goin'. I'm goin' with you." The trooper handcuffed Botchie and locked him in his trunk and took him back to the prison. He was taken directly to the hospital to have his foot tended and was met there by now Major C. J. Burke, the Deputy Warden. He glared down at Botchie with a venomous look in his eyes. "You will regret this day for the rest of your life." Burke then turned on his heel to leave the room, stopping only to give an order to two guards. "Don't let this man out of your sight."

Saint never did find a car to steal while Botchie was hiding in the bushes. He wound up walking nearly all the way to Norristown, a distance of about 15 miles, and finally got a lift early in the morning from two guys on their way to work. Strangely, they didn't notice his clothes. He hid out in an abandoned building for the rest of the day and the next night. Late on the second night out Saint was trudging down the Germantown Pike toward Philadelphia, just north of Chestnut Hill, when a patrol car pulled up beside him. He didn't have a chance. There was a high stone wall beside him and nowhere to run. Two officers jumped from the car, guns drawn and ordered Saint to stop. He stopped, put his hands in the air, and stood absolutely still. Freedom had lasted less than two days.

For their escape attempt Van Sant and Tenuto were charged with Prison Breach, tried at the court house in Norristown, and sentenced to five to ten years. They now owed the state a minimum of 35 years and 25 years respectively. Their efforts, as happens more often than not in these matters, only made matters worse. They were sent to Eastern State Penitentiary and the ante had been increased. This was beginning to look like a life sentence.

———————

Following trial they were shipped to Eastern State Penitentiary on Fairmount Avenue in Philadelphia, supposedly a more secure prison than Graterford. Many escape attempts had been made, but the last successful escape occurred in 1923. Four inmates used a ladder to breach the the walls and one, Leo Callahan, was never recaptured.[1]

Chapter 8

A Whole New Life

A few days after Botchie and Saint were safely back in captivity at Eastern State Penitentiary, Joe Corvi was paroled. Having served his minimum sentence of five years, he left determined not to mess up his life again. He was going to make something of himself. Upon returning to South Philly Joe lived with his sister, Helen, and her husband, Tony, who welcomed him warmly. The Azzatos lived on 10th Street in a three story, brick row home. Figuring out what to do with himself was no problem. The war was in full swing and Joe's big brother, John, as well as numerous friends were serving in Europe. Joining the Army seemed like the right thing to do.

The first stop was the neighborhood draft board. Draft Boards were as thick as weeds in a deserted lot. There was one in nearly every neighborhood and they were run by local people. However, in Corvi's case, the Draft Board people weren't very helpful. He discovered that the U. S. Army didn't want ex-convicts and neither did any other branch of the service. If nobody else was available to induct, which seemed unlikely in a neighborhood full of able-bodied men, and there was a need, he might be taken. He could register for the draft, but wasn't going anywhere soon. On the other hand, there were a lot of jobs available because so many men had gone to war and finding an alternative was easy enough.

The ICS drafting program proved helpful when Joe applied for a job at the Penflex Metal Hose Company located in Southwest Philly at 72nd Street and Powell Lane. The Personnel Manager, who had the personality of a cold stone, spoke in monosyllables and wore a hairpiece, handed Joe a job application, #2 pencil, and gestured to a student desk. Joe slid into the chair, placed the one page form on the writing surface and began filling in the blanks. Except for name, address and telephone number, many of the answers were made up since Joe's work history was nil. He didn't think that experience gained in prison industry was what they were looking for. His brother-in-law was Corvi's sole reference. There were no questions regarding criminal convictions so no information was provided. Next, he was sent to talk with Tom Weaver, the man who would become his boss. He was a short, stout fellow, soft spoken and about 45 years old. When he found out Joe had earned a certificate in Drafting from ICS, he was hired. The starting pay was $80 a week.

Penflex occupied two large brick buildings that faced each other on Powell Lane. Administration was located in one building with departments such as personnel, purchasing and accounting. The same building housed the fitting shop where couplings and other fittings were manufactured. Across the road was the hose manufacturing facility. Joe shared an office with Tom Weaver. Actually, it wasn't really an office, but a space demarcated by partitions that extended to within a foot or so from the ceiling, the 1940s version of open office landscape. Tom had a desk in their little cubicle and Joe worked at a drafting table facing him. The job involved producing engineering drawings, specification sheets and illustrations for the product catalogues.

Tom was impressed with Joe. The new guy's work was neat, he worked fairly fast and never missed a day. The boss was pleased and spoke well of Joe to his superiors. For his part, Joe decided that he should study engineering in order to improve his position with the firm. There was no such thing as a Tuition Reimbursement Program offered at Penflex but Joe, by chance, managed a meeting with Mr. Charles Newhall, who was a member of the Penflex board of directors and formerly the Chairman of a large Philadelphia banking firm. The two men visited briefly and Newhall was impressed with the young man and his initiative. The long and the short of it was that Mr. Newhall agreed to personally reimburse Joe for tuition and books upon receipt of grade cards indicating satisfactory performance.

Joe's routine was working during the day at the plant, attending engineering classes, mostly at night, at Drexel University, and studying whenever he had the opportunity. There must have been ample opportunity because during the two years he attended classes Joe managed to maintain a very respectable 3.5 GPA. At the end of each semester Joe and Mr. Newhall would meet at his office in the factory where Joe would present his grade card. There was very little discussion–maybe a question or two or a compliment for the good work–but Newhall always slid a check across his desk to cover the expenses as promised. The other thing he did was tell management about the bright young man with all the ambition.

Somebody else was singing Joe's praises as well. Helen Azzato thought her little brother was a prize catch and wasn't bashful about telling her unmarried girlfriends all about him. He was handsome, had a good job and was going to college. She wasn't above getting a little aggressive in her matchmaker's role. She also actively promoted those of her friends she thought were "acceptable" to her brother. "Joe," she'd say with a sly twinkle in her eye, "you ought to see my friend Rose. She's a real knock out!" Or maybe it'd be Anne or Virginia. And, on occasion, even if it was just to keep his sister happy, Joe would rise to the bait. Other times it was more like entrapment.

One of Helen's very close, longtime friends was Mary Salvaggio and Mary had a sister-in-law, (an ex-sister-in-law actually) whose name was Esther Ercolain. The two women had become close friends and remained so even after Esther and Mary's brother got divorced. Helen and Mary both thought that Esther and Joe would be a match made in heaven. Finally, this belief turned into a full-blown conspiracy that neither Joe nor Esther knew about until the trap snapped shut.

One Saturday afternoon Helen asked Joe to go over to Mary's with her on the pretext of wanting company. Joe, unsuspecting, agreed readily enough. He liked Mary's family and was tired of studying anyway. When the pair arrived at Mary's row house on Juniper Street, Helen banged on the front door a couple of times and just barged in, Joe right behind her.   There in the living room sitting rather primly was this absolutely, drop dead beautiful girl–Esther. Joe wasn't a shy guy and he wasn't normally at a loss for words either. But for a moment he was struck dumb. *Cheez and crackers*, he said to himself as his eyes took in the sight. Esther had a terrific figure and long, flowing blond hair that framed a delicately beautiful face. She gave new meaning to the word statuesque.

As soon as the introductions were made, Mary and Helen immediately disappeared into some other room in the house and the young couple were left to their own devices. Joe found his voice and started talking about everything–school, his job, the neighborhood. And, he naturally wanted to know all about Esther. She'd been married to Mary's brother, Al, for three years before they separated, but remained a friend of the family. After she was divorced, she found a job in a small women's boutique on Passyunk Avenue where she was a sales clerk.   No, she didn't have a boyfriend, nor was she looking for one at the moment.

Joe listened carefully to all of this and had two thoughts. One, he was glad she didn't have a boyfriend and, two, she was about to get one. He grinned a little impishly and said, "You're way too pretty not to have a boyfriend, but that's up to you. How do you feel about having a plain old friend who's a boy?"

Esther feigned thoughtfulness and finally announced, "Maybe that'd be alright."

The next weekend Joe called her and asked if she'd like to have supper with him at Palumbo's Restaurant, a well known South Philly eatery. She agreed. Helen insisted that Joe use the family car for that first date. She seemed about as excited as Joe was, but was more verbal about it. Joe suggested that given the trap she'd set for him, she ought to rent him a chauffeured limo.

Frank Palumbo's Restaurant was located on the corner of Daren and Catherine Streets.   There was a nice neighborhood restaurant on the first floor and a night club on the second floor with live music and a skylight that could be opened to allow a breeze during the hot summer evenings. The couple had supper downstairs and, later, went up to the club for a drink and a couple of dances.   And that's how it went for the next six months–weekend movies or dancing at some of the nicer clubs around or maybe just a long walk in Fairmount Park down along Boathouse Row. After six months, Joe and Esther were married by a Justice of the Peace in Upper Darby. His younger sister, Marie, and her boyfriend stood up for the couple.

They set up housekeeping in an apartment on 9th and Fitzwater in the Italian section of South Philly. It was a four story, red brick row house with eight apartments, two on each floor. The building had been cloned up and down the street, in fact, all over Philadelphia. Every building had a stoop at the top of a half dozen steps leading up from the street. There was a large door with a glass panel that opened into a small foyer. Eight mailboxes were recessed into the wall to the right. The Corvi's was the rear apartment on the second floor–two bedrooms, a living room and a kitchen. In a little over nine months a new arrival, Jennie, occupied the second bedroom.

Joe continued to work for Penflex for a little over a year. The company was having some financial troubles and, in an effort to trim costs, management brought in some efficiency experts from the Proudfoot Organization in the form of Mr. Packard and his hired guns. Headhunters, that's what they were and they skulked around with clipboards and stop watches, watching what people did, how they did it and who they did it to. Every movement inspired a notation on the clip board. They even noted when employees went to the rest room. It didn't take long for Joe's temper and sharp tongue to get him into trouble.

One of the henchmen, as they were affectionately called, came upon Joe in the restroom one day. The restroom was the only place where the employees could smoke and that's what Joe had been doing. He was about to leave, but noticed the man making a note on his clipboard. This, of course, rankled Joe and he made a remark about some people getting a little too personal. On the very next day there was an employee meeting during which Mr. Packard, with some of Penflex's top management present, explained what he and his people were doing. At some point he intoned, "We're using standard industrial engineering techniques in an effort to improve individual and company performance." Then he went on to explain how the employees could help by behaving normally and ignoring the time study men.

This sounded a lot like a line of bull to Joe Corvi. In his opinion, as well as that of other workers, these guys were goons that the company had brought in to spy on and fire people. Remembering his experience in the restroom the day before, Joe felt compelled to speak up. "Does this study business include following people into the restrooms and counting flushes?" You could have heard a pin drop in the room. Then snickers could be heard around the room. Mr. Packard glared at Joe, who glared right back.   The next day one of Packard's men came into the engineering cubicle and, with no preamble and less explanation, told Joe he was fired, handed him a pay envelope containing the earnings owed him, and escorted him from the building. Joe was plenty mad, but kept calm. No sense in breaking parole and getting sent back to the Farm just for clobbering this clown.

———————

Actually, leaving Penflex was probably one of the better things that ever happened to Corvi. After getting fired at the hose company, Joe took his pay envelope and went to a hangout on 10th and Hall, right across the street from the Ideal Bakery, to play some cards. The bakery specialized in Italian loaves such as cuzzupe at Easter, La Colomba Pasquale, and the standard long loaf. The smells of fresh bread baking were incredible, enough to make a Joe salivate. The gambling den caused a different sort of sensory experience for Joe, who loved the risks and the challenge and was a confirmed and accomplished gambler.

The "den" was actually an empty store that was sort of commandeered by the gambling crowd. On any given day or night action could be found there. The game of choice, called Banker and Broker, required no skill at all aside from moderately nimble fingers and a whole lot of luck. Any player could win the deal only by turning up an ace during play. Or if the dealer tapped out, any player could ask for the deal and get it.

The rules of the game are simple. The deck is shuffled and cut. Then several cards are whisked off the bottom of the deck by the dealer who holds the deck as close to the table as possible. This whisking business is done to ensure that no player has caught a glimpse of the bottom card. The reason will become clear. The cards are not dealt in the normal sense of the word. Instead, the dealer holds the deck between fingers and thumb and literally drops several cards into a pile. There is usually one pile for each broker or player and one for the dealer. The exception is when a single player wishes to play two piles at a time. Piles are chosen by the simple expedient of placing a bet on top of it. The maximum size of a bet allowed is determined by the mutual agreement of the players. The dealer then picks up whichever pile remains after everyone has made a choice and turns it over, exposing the bottom card. Leaving the card exposed, he then takes the money off the pile of one player, beginning at either end of the table. The high card wins and the dealer either collects or pays instantly, before turning to the next pile. Each pile, in turn, is played in the same manner until all piles have been turned. Then the cards are shuffled and the whole process begins again.

As soon as the game he was watching was over, Corvi joined the table, placed his bet and won with an ace. In a single hand he had the bank. He then proceeded to win the entire field three times in a row playing against eight men. One of his rules was to play until he'd either lost whatever limit he'd established before taking a seat or doubled his money. In three games he'd more than doubled his money, he was up over 200 dollars. "Pass the deal," he announced to the other players. He was headed to the door when one loser, a local tough called Hinkey Frank, stopped him.

"Where ya think you're goin'?"

Joe looked at the man and shrugged, "Out that door."

"Not 'til I get a chance at gettin' back some of my money, you ain't."

This wasn't looking good. Joe knew he was going to have to whip this guy to get out of the place and was looking around for some sort of equalizer when another voice spoke up–a big voice.

"Probably ought to leave ole Joe alone," the voice said. "He's a good friend of me and Barney here. Course, ya should do what ya want."

Hinkey Frank took one look at the man with the voice, a very large, powerful looking man with an equally tough looking guy sitting beside him and decided he didn't want to play with Joe anymore. Joe, who thought he'd recognized the voice, looked around to see who his savior was. There sitting on chairs that leaned back against the wall were two acquaintances   from Graterford, Eddie Logan and Barney Brennan. Joe didn't know they were out, but was sure happy to see them, especially given the circumstances.

Later on that day at a local taproom called Recotta's the three Graterford graduates gossiped over a draft. Logan asked, "How long ya been out, Joe?"

"About two years now. Got out right after Botchie and Tenuto went over the wall."

"Yeah, they're both locked at the House now. Burke woulda killed both of 'em if they'd stayed at Graterford."

Barney was a quiet guy. He just sat there nursing his beer and listened. Logan and Joe talked about this and that, like a couple of guys who had gone to the same school together and hadn't seen each other for a long time, which in a way was the case. There was nothing intimate about the conversation. They weren't great friends or anything. They talked about wives and kids, mutual friends, just chit chat. Finally the talk got around to "how ya doin," meaning what are you doing for a living and are you making a living doing it? Joe explained, in a voice that was developing a raspy edge as he aged, all about spies and sneaks and scalp hunters–Mr. Packard and company.

Logan grinned, "Don't like 'em very much, do ya?"

Joe just looked at the man grimly. "Under different circumstances, I'd do a little hunting myself. Not worth it though."

"Barney and me are riggers, Local 161. Why don't ya come to work with us? Good pay, medical, pension and all that stuff."

Joe certainly didn't have any better prospects at the moment. He readily accepted the offer.

Logan introduced Joe to the business agent, a potbellied guy named Griffin, who sent Joe off with a couple of other union guys, maybe shop stewards, to get "interviewed". This was a perfunctory affair, mostly an exchange of baseball scores and bullshit. Background, college experience and employment history were of no interest to these guys. Logan, a member in good standing, had made a recommendation and that was sufficient. Besides, Joe looked healthy and strong and seemed reasonably intelligent, so he got a job earning $10 per hour batting (working) out of the hall.

The work was wonderful. Joe had found his niche in a business that was both physical and mentally challenging. The business has a lingo all its own, one foreign to anybody who doesn't work in the trade. There were terms like luffs and lifting lines; sling chains and snatch blocks; tail holds and twisters. The men worked with heavy lift equipment such as winches and A-frames and lattice boom cranes. The companies the riggers worked for, like Frank W. Hake Rigging and Transporting, moved really big equipment such as 100 ton transformers and huge generators. Other companies moved lathes and presses. Every job was unique and presented its own problems and challenges.

The riggers usually went on jobs in gangs of four. One man was assigned the foreman's position, which only meant he got the rate, not that he bossed anybody. The guys usually knew their jobs very well and everybody performed. One day you'd work with one gang and the next, maybe, with three different guys. The problem with the profession, like others in the building trades, was that the work wasn't always steady. A man might work two months on a job and then be laid off for a week or two. The rigger who was out of work the longest always got the next job, but that didn't make up for lost time. That was okay with Joe though, he looked forward to every day and loved it.

And, as a result of generally good pay, Joe had a good life and managed to save a few bucks for a rainy day. He went out for a beer once in a while or shot some crap with the guys– his one bad habit. He really enjoyed gambling. The risk and challenge was like manna to him. Mostly, however, Joe's social life was with his wife and little girl. Weekday evenings were generally spent at home or maybe visiting friends or neighbors. On Sundays the family would have dinner with Esther's family or his sister Helen. Either that or company would come to their home. These gatherings were casual affairs full of small talk and laughter. For the most part, Joe was comfortable. He had a good job, his wife was doing well, and they had what they wanted in life.

———————

There was only one dark cloud hanging on the horizon and things were going so well that Joe was beginning to worry about it. That cloud was spelled **p a r o l e**. If Joe messed up–cold-cocked some smart aleck for mouthing off to his wife, was arrested for gambling or was found having a beer with Eddie and Barney or anybody else who had graduated from the state prison system–it was life's over. He'd be sent back to Graterford to finish up his term, 15 more years. Joe heard about an attorney, Claude Berman, who had successfully represented ex-cons before the Pardon Board at Harrisburg and had gotten their paroles commuted. That meant the last 15 years would be erased, just like it had never existed.

Lawyer Berman was an impressive looking guy, well built and a good dresser. He listened attentively to Joe's recitation of his more recent history, scratching a few notes on a yellow legal pad. "Joe," he said, "you've got a good story to tell: over three years of good behavior, a good job and a family. Everything suggests you've got your life straightened out. I think we've got a good chance for a commutation." He paused for effect before continuing. "Of course, you never know. I've seen some very favorable petitions rejected. We don't win them all."

Joe, ever the optimist, just brushed the disclaimer aside. "Let's go for it, all they can say is no."

Within a month a petition had been submitted and Joe and Mr. Berman were before the Pardons Board with the lawyer stating the case. The state's Attorney General was there, acting as the chairman, along with a bunch of other dignitaries Joe had never heard of. The hearing was brief. Berman recounted Joe's history since being released on parole–good behavior, job and family. The pair was dismissed while the board discussed the case and, in a few minutes were asked to return to the hearing room. The petition was granted and Joe was truly a free man.

If there was one thing Corvi would have liked better, it was a year round job–steady work with a little more security than a man enjoyed batting out of the hall. The opportunity came when Joe was assigned to a crew of riggers helping to install a new printing press for the Philadelphia Inquirer at the company's printing plant on Broad Street and Callowhill. It was a huge job–20, 13-ton units had to be lifted off flat bed trucks onto chain blocks and rollers, moved onto steel rails and, finally, skidded into place for the millwrights to connect. In the process of performing the work, Joe discovered there was a good bit of rigging work going on in a plant all the time. He offered his services and was told they would consider hiring him. The newspaper would have a captive rigger and a known quantity instead getting a different man from the hall every time there was work to be done. For Joe, it would be the best of two worlds. He'd remain a member of Local 161, earning union wages and benefits, and also would have a 52 week a year job. Things were looking up for the Corvis.

That afternoon Joe met Eddie Logan at the union hall and offered to buy him a beer while he told him about his good fortune. Joe didn't want to get into trouble with the union and Eddie could help pave the way. The two men nursed a beer while Joe told his friend about the deal the newspaper was considering. They were discussing the pros and cons as well as any possible union objections when a third man interrupted them.

"You're Joe Corvi, ain't ya?" he asked.

Joe looked at the man, recognized the face, but didn't know why. "Yeah." he replied.

The man grinned and stuck out his hand. "I'm Jack Moribito. Thought I remembered ya. Didn't mean to bother youse guys. Why don't ya come visit me a minute b'fore ya leave."

Joe nodded, still puzzled about who the man was. As it turned out, Eddie remembered him. "That guy's from Graterford, Joe. Don't know him, just remember seein' him around."

The friends talked a little bit longer and Eddie left. Joe took the remains of his beer and walked over to the table where Moribito was sitting with a couple of other guys. The other fellows left immediately when Joe arrived, leaving him and Moribito alone.

Moribito was a short, solidly built man with a lined face and graying hair cropped short.

He looked into his beer glass a moment and then said, "Don't remember me do ya?"

"Remember the face, but not you. Don't think we did anything but time together. Eddie, the guy I was sitting with, remembered you–from the Farm." After a pause, Joe, impatient, said, "What can I do for you."

Moribito, looked at him seriously for a moment. It's the other way 'round, what I kin do for you. Got a story to tell."

Joe, sat back in his chair, arms folded across his chest. He had a bad feeling about this conversation.

"Never would've thought of this, except I saw ya t'day. Knew ya by reputation. Ya may not be interested at all, up ta you." He paused a second. Joe just sat there and didn't say anything. He should have left right then.

"Friend of mine works for a contractor doin' some work up on the Mainline, Waterloo Road. Huge houses, manicured lawns and stuff. There's the rich n' the filthy rich–then there's the people living in this house. Said there was stuff laying all over the place, expensive stuff like silver and pictures and diamonds and things. Said the lady of the house was a social butterfly or somethin'. Wears a fortune on herself just bummin' 'round the house. Name is Von Bosig, Von Boren or somethin' like that."

Moribito stopped talking and looked at Joe, who looked like a sphinx. "Just thought ya might be interested."

"Yeah, thanks." Joe walked off muttering to himself. *Cheez and crackers.*

———————

Just a few weeks later Joe and Esther were out on the town. It was one of those memorable times, a special time, and they were celebrating their good fortune. He'd gotten the job at the Inquirer. They had it made! Tonight, with Jennie safe at Grandma's house, Joe and his best girl were seated at The Click, Frank Palumbo's club down on Market Street and perhaps one of the swankiest in town. This was the place of the social elite and local celebrities. They were holding hands over the table and listening to a male vocalist singing "The House I Live In," which was made famous by the very popular and boyish Frank Sinatra. Billie Holliday, the famous lady jazz singer, who was born in Philadelphia, sometimes performed here. Tonight, they would dance to some of Holliday's hit tunes–"Easy Living" and "Yesterdays" that were made popular during the late 1930s.

The young couple were completely entranced with each other as they danced, listened to the music, and held hands. They had toasted their lives and good fortune and then had nursed the same drink all evening long while they talked about their future and that of Jennie. It was a grand night. They were in love and they felt good.

———————

More and more there was this nagging, insinuating thought in the back of Joe's head. It was about Moribito's mansion out on Waterloo Road. One of those that looked like it should be standing on an English country estate in an earlier century, with a Tudor-style house and a carriage house and formal gardens with marble statuary. One of those castle-like affairs filled with treasure. He dreamed of fabulous jewels and stacks of thousand dollar bills and a hoard of priceless artifacts like medieval jeweled goblets and Fabergé Easter eggs. But it wasn't so much the treasure that was taunting him. That was only the prize. It was the thrill of taking an extraordinary, almost primordial risk, maybe like hunting a savage beast with primitive weapons or free climbing an impossible rock wall or rafting a class five rapid. It was the challenge of breaching the walls of a mythical monster's castle, stealing his most valued possession, and escaping undetected.

These were the inexplicable feelings that had landed Joe Corvi behind bars twice before. They were the same feelings that took him to Waterloo Road one night in mid-October of 1944. He had looked under Von in the telephone directory until he found one listed on Waterloo Street. It was VonBergen. The Chester County court house provided an address and property description. The house was built in 1905 and located on a real country estate with over 20 acres surrounding it. Horace Trumbauer, the favored architect of Philadelphia's wealthy elite during his time, had designed the mansion. Corvi had seen one of Trumbauer's creations when it starred in the film *The Philadelphia Story* which also featured Katharine Hepburn, Cary Grant and James Stewart.[1]

The house was three stories with lights on in only the lower two. Joe crept up to one of the lighted windows on the ground floor and peered into what appeared to be a formal living room. There were paneled walls, sculpted plaster ceilings and, at one end, what looked like a hand-carved fireplace. Nobody was in the room. Two people, a man and a woman, were in the next room, which was more like a den or a library. Bookshelves covered the wall facing the window. A huge hardwood door with ornate, shiny, brass hardware split the bookshelves into two sections. The woman was reading something, maybe a magazine, and she glittered beneath the lights–the glitter was the light reflecting off the jewelry she was wearing. She was attractive and maybe forty or so with blond hair. The man, presumably her husband, was dressed casually, wearing a sweater and slippers. The furniture looked comfortable, but expensive, and the carpeting was something a man could simply disappear into walking across the floor.

Backing away from the window, Corvi crept around the house with care. Wherever there was a light he looked in the window. Any of the windows, except those facing the circular driveway, would make a good access. He searched carefully for any sign of an alarm system and failed to find anything. Still, he was worried. A house this size and with such obvious wealth was bound to have an alarm. Finally he left. Another recon trip would be necessary.

In the course of a two week period. Joe made three trips around the house and several drive-bys. During one of the trips, on a Friday night, nobody was home. He used a flash light to closely examine the windows and doors for signs of wiring or a siren. Nothing. He did manage to discover two sets of stairs leading to the second floor and an entry point, a window on the west side of the house, that was partially shielded by a large bush.

On the next Friday night he returned, ready to get on with his job. The previous Friday visit and several drive-bys suggested that Friday night was a regular night out. He parked his Studebaker among some trees on a deserted lane about a half mile away and stood there long enough for his eyes to adjust to the dark. Then he made his way toward the house, approaching across a meadow and through a copse of trees. His nerves had a fine edge and, although perfectly calm, he felt strangely exhilarated. Well, perhaps not strangely, he always felt like this when approaching a job. The adrenalin rush would come as he made his escape. It had been a long time since he'd had this feeling.

Joe paused several times as he approached the house, listening carefully for animals or any telltale noise. All was quiet. He slipped behind the bush and stood outside the window waiting for a moment, listening and looking in. A jimmy bar, one of those short pry bars, was all Joe carried with him. He didn't like flash lights, because they could be seen through the windows. Nor was there a sack of any kind, he took with him only what could be carried in his pockets.

He slipped the tapered head of the jimmy bar between the sill and the bottom rail of the double-hung window and applied an upward force. The window wouldn't budge, probably a sash lock. Joe checked his purchase, took a breath and applied a powerful surge of force. He could feel the screws pop loose and the window slid up smoothly.

Once inside he stood still again, listening. The house was silent, made the more so by the heavy carpeting. Satisfied that he was alone, Joe got his bearings and began to move toward where the stairway was located. He moved slowly seeing dim forms and shapes in the little bit of light filtering through the windows. His path took him through the den and into the kitchen. Then he proceeded down a hallway toward the front of the house. Several minutes had elapsed from the time he forced the window until he finally arrived at the stairs.

———

The moment Joe forced the window a pressure sensitive circuit contact between the upper and lower sash rail was broken. On a panel located in the basement a red light began flashing and a tape dialer was activated. A phone rang at the Tredyffrin Township police department. When the dispatcher answered the phone, a taped message alerted him to a potential security problem at 1050 Waterloo Road. The closest patrol car was immediately dispatched to that address.

———

As Joe began to climb the stairs a light flashed through the windows on either side of the heavy front door. Quickly, he hurried to the window and peered out. "Cheez and crackers." The police car pulled around the circular drive and stopped in front of the house. A spot light played over the front of the house and on the front door. After a moment's pause, probably to report that he had arrived, an officer got out of the car with a flashlight in hand, walked to the front entry and rang a very loud doorbell. Joe stood silently behind the door. Satisfied that nobody was going to answer the door, the policeman turned away and began to walk a circuit around the house looking for a point of entry. Joe sat down on a small chair that was in the foyer and calmly smoked a cigarette while he waited. He should have closed the window behind him.

When the dust settled and the court got done with him, Joe Corvi owed the Commonwealth of Pennsylvania another 10 to 20 years. His decision to apply for a commutation of his parole only six months earlier displayed great prescience. Had that request been rejected Corvi would have been facing a minimum of 25 years, the 15 left on the previous sentence followed by at least ten years of the new sentence. After being sent to Eastern State in Philadelphia for classification, he was sent back to Graterford for a time, but finally wound up back in the House, assigned to cell block 8. The Saint and Botchie were locked in 7 Block.

Chapter 9

Third Trip Up the River

Joe Corvi was sitting on his cot in B-Block at Graterford Prison holding his head in his hands like a man with a monstrous hangover. His butt and his mood were in the same shape, black and blue, and it was all self-inflicted. When Joe told his wife, Esther, what he'd done, that he'd screwed up again, the tears welled up in her eyes and streamed down her cheeks. It nearly killed him. There were no complaints or self-pity over being caught that night on Waterloo Road. He'd been caught red-handed and there would be no whining about the penalty. But he deeply regretted what he'd done to Esther and their daughter. Her tears and the stricken look were indelibly etched in his mind and burned into his soul. He thought about that every day.

He'd spent the usual time at the House getting printed, mugged, classified, analyzed and, following the usual protocol, assigned the first available cell. That happened to be at The Farm, Graterford. Once again he was assigned a number–damned number, faceless number, impersonal number. Once again a caged cipher. That number, E-939, was nothing more than the newest statistic on a list that began ten or twelve years earlier when the maximum security prison first opened its arms to the bad guys of eastern Pennsylvania. Two guards escorted Corvi through a heavy steel door, followed by a second barred door, followed by another. Each door shut with a single, metallic, echoing clank. Corvi and his escort walked down the quarter mile long main corridor to B-

Block, his new home. This was the first day of the rest of his life, or at least, he thought, of the next ten years.

New arrivals at prison were usually assigned to a labor detail. For Joe and some other men that involved picking up loose paper and other detritus discarded in the exercise yard by the inmates. After a short time Joe found himself working for Mr. McQuade, who supervised the construction crew. As it turned out, the job didn't last very long. On the first day it poured down rain and the workers were confined to the cell block. The same on the second. On the third day the crew, including Corvi, was led out to the construction site where the men were instructed to pick a tool out of the gang box. Then they were led to a seven feet deep and four feet wide ditch which was awash in all the water collected from the previous two days of rain.

Mr. McQuade, a burly man in his fifties, called out in a loud voice, "Okay, this is it. Get down there and get rid of that water."

Everyone clamored down into the ditch as ordered. Everyone except Joe Corvi, who just stood there with a shovel propped under his arm. It was a first class impression of insolence and insubordination.

"Hey, you," the foreman demanded impatiently. "You waitin' for a special invitation?"

Joe looked at the man for a couple of seconds. "I've no intention of going into that hole."

"Well, you'll either get inta the hole or you'll get assigned to Klondike. Maybe that'll suit ya better."

"You won't be getting a virgin."

Thirty days later Joe was released back to his normal cell block and was promptly taken to see Deputy Warden David N. Meyers, who at the time was also acting Warden.

Meyers was a big, gruff, ex-state cop. Not a friendly sort at all, he'd walk by an inmate like he was a post. Probably necessary behavior, given the place. When Corvi arrived in Meyer's office, he was at his desk. He never looked up and didn't offer Joe a chair. Abruptly, he looked up and began talking. "So ya won't work eh?"

"Didn't say I wouldn't work, Sir. Just won't work in a ditch full of water. Besides, bailing water out of a ditch isn't going to teach me anything of any value for when I'm released."

Meyer looked at Joe speculatively and sighed. "Okay, I'll start you out as a stock clerk in the tailor shop. Ya know where that is, don't ya?

"Yes, Sir."

"You can report there right now."

That was the end of the meeting. One of the office clerks, Nick Cardone, handed Joe a piece of paper with some scribbles on it. Accompanied by a guard, off Joe went to the tailor shop. Clerking was better than bailing water, but still mind-numbing. It was something to do, though. Another opportunity presented itself a few months later. One of Meyers' clerks, Ollie Olson, was paroled and Nick Cardone, who Joe had become friends with, asked if he would like to work with him in the bull's office. The answer was, "Of course." Nick agreed to take care of it.

A couple of days later Meyers asked Nick, who was the head clerk, who he would like to have work with him. "If ya got a minute, I'll bring his file," Nick replied. The file was already on Nick's desk in readiness. He carried the file to Meyers' desk and laid it in front of him. The Major opened the folder and there was a picture of Joe Corvi staring back at him. His head snapped up. "What! Are you nuts! No way." Two more days passed and the same question asked. Same answer, same response. Nick had to report to Corvi that it didn't look too good.

"Look, Nick, I appreciate your help," Corvi said, "but maybe I should talk to Meyers myself."

Nick shrugged and said, "Submit a request." Usually when a request for an interview is made, the inmate is summoned to the office. Not so in this case.

Later on that day Meyers showed up in the stock room. He leaned on one of the stock cabinets and beckoned to Joe with his head. Joe walked over and assumed a similar position on the other side of the cabinet.

"What do ya want Corvi?"

"I want to work In your office, for Cardone, Sir."

Meyer just shook his head. "With your temper, you'd never make it. One of the guards would set you up and you'd land back in Klondike."

"I think I can control my temper, Major. Why not give me a shot at it? I'll do a good job for you."

Meyers looked at him for a long moment before responding. "You better stay where you're at."

That should have been that, but, inexplicably, on the following Monday morning, in the tailor shop, the phone rang. The clerk yelled, "Corvi, you're wanted up front. At the office, Corvi stood before Major Meyers, Bill Banmiller, who would later become the Warden at Eastern State Penitentiary, and the other Deputy Warden, Major Maske. The three officers, three among others who Joe would be working for if he got the job, grilled him for 30 minutes. Joe, suppressing the urge to offer some smart aleck response, played it straight. One question asked was, "An inmate asks you for help getting a particular job and you accommodate him. The man is awarded the job and later tries to give you five packs of cigarettes. Do you take the cigarettes? Of course, everybody thought they knew what would really happen, but Joe answered, "I don't think that would be proper, Sir."

At the end of the meeting Joe was asked to leave the office and the three officers caucused behind the closed door. In a few minutes Meyers came out of his office, nodded at Joe, turned to his head clerk and said, "Nick, put this guy to work will ya."

––––––––––

The clerk's duties involved all the usual stuff like filing, answering the phone and scheduling inmate interviews. One important function was liaison between the Sergeants and Meyers on job assignments. Sometimes Joe interceded. Occasionally an inmate would approach him looking for an outside job that paid a little more than 15 or 20 cents a day. If there extenuating circumstances, such as family hardship or a sick mother, Joe would help the inmate get a Department of Welfare job that paid as much as $15 per month. This was usually accomplished by placing the favored inmate's file on the top of the pile. Meyers would invariably accept Joe's choice, apparently feeling his clerk knew the people better than he did. Another of Joe's responsibilities was keeping files of all misconducts and typing misconduct reports. It was a little difficult in the beginning, especially typing the reports.

One morning shortly after Joe became a clerk, Captain Johnson came into the office and asked Joe to type up a misconduct report for him as he dictated it. Joe looked at the Captain, and without missing a beat, said, "Yes, Sir." He sat down in front of an old Remington, poised his hands over the worn keys in apparent readiness, and glanced at the Captain. The Captain nodded and began talking in a normal voice and Corvi's hands glided effortlessly over the keys. The typewriter clattered and Joe looked at the Captain a little strangely. The Captain kept on dictating and Corvi's hands kept gliding. In a few minutes the officer pronounced the report complete. Joe pulled the paper from the typewriter and handed it over. A look of puzzlement and incomprehension covered the Captain's face and his brow furrowed. Then he fairly sputtered, "What to hell is this?"

"It's the best I can do, Captain. Sorry," Joe replied apologetically. The Captain looked at Joe and at the sheet of paper. It was an alphabet soup of black letters floating around on the white page in complete disorder. Joe didn't know how to type. The Captain, for a moment, stood there bewildered and speechless. Then he took up a pen, signed his name to the completely unintelligible mess and turned to leave. He paused and looked at Corvi with a wry smile, "You'd better do something about your little problem pretty quick, Corvi." And Joe did. Within a month he could type. He wouldn't win any competition and the work wasn't always error free, but he could type.

Joe worked for Major Meyers for about two years. From day one, the Major trusted Corvi completely and, in turn, the inmate never abused his position. He did indeed help some inmates get a better paying job if there was a good reason. But he never did take cigarettes for the favor. Meyer never regretted hiring Joe and Joe never regretted taking the job.

All this happiness and the bliss came to an end with the arrival of A. T. Rundle, who replaced Major Maske when the latter retired. A new policy had been established in the Pennsylvania Penal System. That was, no man could hold the position of Deputy Warden or above unless he had a college degree. Maske probably didn't even have a high school diploma. He, like many of the men in high administrative positions, got there by dint of long experience and on-the-job-training. Anyway, when Maske left, Rundle, who was a former school teacher, took his place. It wasn't long before everyone on staff was aware that the new arrival knew absolutely nothing about penology, criminal psychology or human nature. On top of these obvious deficiencies, the man was given to dismissive gestures, condescending remarks and cerebral blather. He was, thought Joe Corvi and many others, an arrogant twit.

Of course, such negative feelings are fairly transparent to anyone with even a modicum of intelligence and so it wasn't long before Major Rundle got the message–he was not held in particularly high esteem by either his colleagues or the inmates. This, of course, resulted in even worse behavior. One day, after a month or so, Rundle came blustering into the office and started rummaging in the file cabinets. Joe, who was observing the activity, asked if he could help the Major find something.

Rundle shot Joe a withering look and announced for all to hear, "I'm perfectly capable of finding anything that I need without any help from you, Corvi." Then unaccountably, he continued, "I'm well aware of your little deceits and scams . . . selling jobs and favors to these ignorant miscreants. I've no idea how you inveigled your way into this office, but if it were up to me you'd be gone." At that, the good Major slammed the filing cabinet drawer shut and stalked out of the office. That was probably the best thing he could have done for everyone concerned. The other clerks listened, both anxious and amazed. At first, Corvi was simply stunned but then became infuriated. Had Rundle not left, there is little doubt that he would have spent some time in the prison infirmary and that Corvi would have spent the remainder of his sentence in solitary confinement.

At the first opportunity Joe told Major Meyers what had happened. The Major, who had no more use for Rundle than anyone else, first listened in disbelief and then got mad as hell. He stormed into the office that he shared with Rundle and slammed the door shut behind him. The sounds of shouts and obscenities could easily be heard. This storm continued for some time until Meyers came busting out of the office red-faced and stiff-legged. Stalking out of the office, he crossed the main corridor and took a position looking out of a window into an exercise area. His arms were windmilling violently and he was raving almost incoherently.

Within a week Joe was reassigned to Eastern State. During a final private conversation, Major Meyers explained his action. "Joe, I got no choice. If I don't get you outa here, that son-of-a-bitch is goin' ta get you." The two men shook hands and Joe left. It was June 1944.

Chapter 10

There's Always a First Time

Back at The House, Joe was locked in 8 Block and had a private cell. His first job was working for Dr. Israel Hyatt as a clerk-typist. Hyatt was the staff psychologist and later went to work at St. Joseph University up on City Line Avenue in Philly. He was responsible for performing evaluations of all entering inmates and also provided professional care for resident inmates. Joe scheduled appointments, took care of correspondence and did all the typing and filing. One of his favorite jobs was administering and scoring the Stanford-Binet test for all men applying for guard positions.

There was a problem in the work force. The war had syphoned off many of the able-bodied men in the country. But there was also a war industry to support. And while Rosie the Riveter filled many of the industry jobs, so did many of the males who for some reason or other couldn't serve in the armed forces. Those jobs payed much better than a guard job in the penitentiary, so there was a chronic shortage of guards during the war. In addition, the quality of men the prisons did manage to hire was often substandard. "Some of the guys I tested," Corvi said, "could hardly tie their own shoes. That might be an overstatement, but they weren't mensa candidates either. Many of 'em were hired anyway."

One time Joe got a live one to deal with, a discharged Marine who arrived in dress blues, bemedalled, and shining like a new penny. This guy was a little troubled over the fact that a blue suited inmate had administered his test in the first place. Joe was evaluating the results when the man began to ask questions.

"When I came in here, I noticed a lot of convicts wandering around unattended. Isn't that dangerous?"

Joe smiled his very best rascally smile. "There's a bunch of inmates wandering around because this's a prison. There's more than a thousand of them locked up here."

"I mean, there were no guards that I could see, except the guy escorting me to your office. Don't these guys give you problems?"

Joe was enjoying the interaction. This guy was way too straight-ahead. "Well, they can't get out easily. The front door isn't accessible and the walls are at least 30 feet high. Besides, if somebody messes up, they're thrown in the hole. It's not a nice place to while away your time."

"This place is more like a resort than a brig. In a Navy brig the prisoners toe the line, speak when spoken to, and ask permission to blow their nose. And they don't go anywhere without a Marine escort. Military discipline prevails."

Now Joe was grinning widely. He leaned back in his chair and could see that both his actions and answers were disturbing the young man. "This isn't a military base or brig, whatever you call it. Our treatment of inmates is more humane."

Joe stood up suddenly and the Marine tensed. "Come on," Joe said, "I'll escort you to the doctor's office for your medical."

That did it. That graduate jarhead didn't want anything to do with a place where the prisoners did the escorting. As they were crossing the center, the Marine abandoned Joe and walked over to the Captain, who was sitting in the control center. "Sir, would you please have someone take me out to the gate. I want out of this place." On his way down the corridor he was muttering something about the inmates running the asylum.

The job in the psychologist's office didn't last very long. Joe made an unauthorized call from the office phone to inquire about his cash account. That earned him some time in solitary, 15 Block. He thought of the Marine candidate.

By the time he got out of solitary, the Hyatt job was already filled and Joe went to work in the pin business. That is, he prepared safety pins and bobby pins and distributed them to other inmates who carded them in their cells during off hours. The carded pins were then returned to the manufacturer and from there were distributed to retail stores for sales. Joe earned about $40 per month doing this work, not bad for convict labor.

When Corvi arrived at Eastern State from Graterford, both Botchie and Saint had already been there for a couple of years and were locked in 7 Block. The men resumed a nodding acquaintance during yard out, but otherwise spent no time together. One of the reasons was that the men from 7 Block were busy.

When the two escapees arrived they received neither special consideration nor sympathy from Herbert 'Bozo' Smith, who had been the warden of Eastern State since 1928[1]. Bozo , as he was known at least to the inmates, was a boozer with the telltale florid-face. For an ex-state trooper, the warden wasn't a large man, only 5'10" and drifting to a little fat. He wasn't a bad guy which means he was fair to all as long as he was treated likewise. On the other hand, Smith had little time for nonsense and was considered a strict disciplinarian. As was the custom, the warden met with Van Sant and Tenuto when they first arrived from Graterford.

"You guys mind your own business, keep your noses clean and do as you're told.

Behave and we'll get along. But if you screw up, you've had it." He paused to let that sink in. "This's a maximum security prison and I've got nearly a 1000[2] inmates as bad or worse than you guys, so you're no big deal to me." Smith turned to leave and then, reconsidering, turned back. "One more thing, I know you guys are going to try and break out. My advice is don't. There's been maybe 30 or 40 attempts on my watch, thirty of 'em tried to burrow out like god damned moles. None were successful," he paused again. "But they all got to spend a lot of time in the Klondike contemplating their sins."

Once the two men had received their 'orientation' from Bozo and passed through the classification process, they were assigned as cell block workers in 7 Block. Block workers were essentially housekeepers who mopped floors on the block, removed trash, and picked up and delivered the inmates' laundry. This was not the most stimulating work in the prison and, normally, both men would have requested a transfer to any one of a number of shops that operated in the prison—a barber shop in nearly every block, leather work, wood working and, of course, the normal maintenance functions such as laundry, car repair and plant maintenance. However, as fate would have it, they first became acquainted with Clarence (Kliney) Klinedinst.

———————

Kliney had a rap sheet 20 years long. Now, at age 38, he was serving his third stretch at Eastern, five and a half to eleven years for burglary. In addition, he owed the remainder of a previous term, seven and a half to eleven years, for breaking parole.[3] A very ordinary man, he was wrapped in plain brown, was ploddingly persistent, thorough, patient, introverted and physically unremarkable—180 pounds, 5' 10", and balding. This description might fit a person with few, if any, friends and who essentially was a loner. Right on both counts. Kliney could walk down the middle of the block cluttered with inmates and neither see nor speak to a single person. He had one great strength, though. He was a first class maintenance man and that earned him an enormous amount of freedom in The House allowing him to go just about anywhere in the prison without question.

He became a nodding acquaintance of Botchie and Saint as a result of asking them for help finding a piece of clothing that hadn't been returned from the laundry. The missing garment, a shirt that had his number stenciled on it, was found and from that point on Kliney nodded if he walked by Botchie and Saint while they were sweeping the cell block. Months of nodding passed before he spoke to the block workers again. Botchie and Saint were walking by Kliney's cell when he stepped out, looked up and down the block to make sure no one was watching, and then asked them to step inside. The two men were understandably curious about what Kliney wanted because this guy didn't talk to hardly anybody. They stepped inside his cell.   Silent Kliney, after a moment's hesitation, got right to the point. "Would you guys be interested in an escape plan I've got?"

The two men were utterly amazed. Of course they were interested, but totally unprepared for either the question or the source of the opportunity–if it was indeed an opportunity. They looked at each other, their eyes saying, *Is this guy for real?*

"Look, I can't tell ya about it now, there's not time and this ain't the place. Too many people. But I can tell ya I've already dug one tunnel half way outa here. Ya know there's tunnels, really maintenance shafts, under this whole place. It's like a rabbit warren down there. How'd ya think they get heat an water an lights inta the blocks? There's a tool room attached to one of the maintenance shafts an that's where I started my tunnel from. Problem was it was too far from the wall, so I quit. Put all the dirt back and sealed up the hole so's nobody'd notice. But all I've been thinkin' about since is tunnels. Think I've solved the problem."

Kliney paused and looked at the two men, first one and then the other, as if trying to hear what they were thinking. "Look, we can't talk here any longer. If you're interested, we'll meet during yard out and I'll tell you the plan."

"That'll be a tough job, friend," Saint replied. "Nobody's dug out of Eastern before that I know about. Heard of one guy trying to get out through the sewer, but he didn't make it. Bozo mentioned a lot of guys trying to dig out, but they didn't make it. But if you got a plan, we're sure interested in hearing it."

For the next several days the duo was on pins and needles. Although a little skeptical, they were more than a little interested in getting out. After a day or two, the men began to think that Kliney had changed his mind or that they had offended him. Finally, they were invited to join the 'silent one' in a game of dominoes during yard out. The meeting took place outside of 8 Block in an abandoned Bocce court.

They sat on a bench facing each other with a three-foot square piece of plywood resting on their laps. Botchie played and Saint looked on. Hundreds of schemes and plans and intrigues had probably been discussed over a game of dominoes but it was far from simple. For one thing, there was always the stray kibitzer coming around, which ended all meaningful conversation.

With his head down, as if concentrating on the game, Kliney began his story. "My last tunnel failed because the distance between the tool room and the wall was too great. What ya want is the shortest distance possible. As far as I can see, the shortest length is from the end of 7 Block, right behind me, to the wall. I'd guess that's about 100 feet. The exit would be on Fairmount Avenue right below the guard tower, in their blind spot. The great thing is that the last cell in 7 Block, cell number 68, is empty. It's the dirt cell where all the trash and garbage collected from the block is stored. Hell, youse guys know all about that, you doin' the collectin'."

In the course of several domino games the plan unfolded. Kliney would proposition the Deputy Superintendent into letting him rehab that dirt cell in exchange for keeping it his own private cell. The prison population was becoming so crowded that some inmates had cell mates. It was well known that Kliney didn't like company so his request made sense. Cell number 57, Kliney's current abode, would become a double cell, so the institution gained space for at least two additional prisoners. Long story short, the DEP approved the plan, providing that Kliney did the work on his own time. The maintenance chief, Albert Dunlap, was instructed to provide any materials needed and the guards were alerted to the plan. All needed materials would be provided by the maintenance shop or 'appropriated' as Dame Opportunity presented. They would need things like saw blades, scrap lumber and electric wire. These various items would be stolen and stored by all three team members in readiness for later use. Botchie and Saint were now enthusiastic conspirators in the plot to go under the wall.

The first order of business was stripping decades of whitewash off the walls and exposing the gray stone blocks underneath. Kliney was quite an actor. He began removing the whitewash, which was inches thick and almost like plaster, in the noisiest and messiest way possible. The cell block officer rushed to the cell door, out of which spewed a cloud of whitish dust, and peered in cautiously. What he saw was Kliney stripped to the waist and streaming sweat as he stood in a whitish-gray cloud, swinging a heavy sledge hammer against the plaster-like substance covering the wall. He had a rag tied about his nose and mouth to filter the dust. The hammer almost rang against the granite stone wall as each blow fell.

The guard interrupted the work. "Klinedinst, dammit, get a wet blanket or something and hang it over this opening. You're making a hell-of-a mess on the block with all this dust."

"Yes sir," was the reply. Just what the doctor ordered–a little privacy from prying eyes. All that was needed now was a lookout and Botchie and Saint could handle that duty.

Under cover of the privacy offered by the wet blanket hanging over the cell door, Kliney began removing the large stone blocks from the wall where he planned the tunnel opening–on the right of the cell door in the corner, where it would be difficult for a curious guard to see while checking the work. Each of the stones was demolished with the sledgehammer. The broken pieces were collected in a 30-gallon trash can. Each morning a dump truck made the rounds of the blocks and picked up the trash. Seven Block was the last on the route so the truck was full of trash by the time it arrived and the noise of the falling chunks of rock was muffled by the other material. And, of course, the block's trash was dumped by Botchie and Tenuto–the block workers. The driver never got out of the truck cab and, since 7 Block was the end of the line, the trash was immediately hauled off to the municipal dump.

On Kliney went, removing stone and the plaster-like white wash, mixing the two and depositing the mess into the trash can. A mortar board, for mixing plaster, was kept in the cell and used to cover the hole being chipped into the wall. Either Saint or Botchie would stay close to the cell and if someone approached, would warn Kliney, who would immediately cover the hole. Once the white wash was all removed, the plastering began. Gouging a hole through the stone in the wall was difficult and time consuming. To account for the extra time, Kliney plastered the walls and allowed chunks of plaster to harden and fall off so parts of the wall had to be re-plastered. And, of course, he also had to attend to his normal maintenance responsibilities.

Once the tunnel entrance was completed, the hole was squared with mortar and a wooden frame installed. Then a box-like hatch was built that would fit snugly into the hole. The frame and hatch were constructed so that the door, when in place, fit flush with the wall and was painted to look exactly the same as the walls. The hatch's sides were even beveled so that the joint between wood and plaster was neither observable nor easily discovered. Further, Kliney scored the walls of the cell all the way around to match the joints of the tunnel hatch. A final touch was screwing a metal waste basket to the hatch cover to further disguise it.

From the entrance, a shaft descended through more stone at an angle away from the building foundation, until Kliney was digging in the soil directly under his own cell. He'd have to dig down to the footing before the actual tunneling could begin. A ladder made of pilfered lumber and discarded benches was used to climb in and out of the shaft and was made longer as depth required. The excavation proceeded at a rate of one to six inches per day, but not every day was a work day. The usual routine had to be maintained lest someone notice and got nosy.

The digging was accomplished with makeshift tools, discarded tools and stolen tools–a worn out shovel carelessly tossed aside, chisels and trowels pilfered from the shop and even an old scrub-bucket cut in two with mop handles attached for spare shovels. Before they were done, they'd need lumber for cribbing, about 100 feet of electrical wire, plus who knows what else. The fill from the shaft was disposed of through normal prison trash hauling as had been done with the rock and whitewash. In all, about a month had elapsed since Kliney began the project in April 1944, now it was May and the tunnel level was yet to be reached. However, Kliney could now work standing up in the shaft.

It was time for Kliney to set up housekeeping in his new domicile. The cell was painted, as was the bed, foot locker and bench. He even gave himself an added reward, a small writing desk located right next to the tunnel access. The only light in the cell was directly over the desk.

Throughout the "construction" the cell block guards had dropped in from time to time and looked on in amazement. Now the transformation was complete and what a transformation it was. The cell block guards persuaded Deputy Warden Martin to take a look.

Kliney stood next to his bunk, where he'd been resting when the DEP appeared. Martin stood in the middle of the cell looking around, clearly impressed. He even looked into the waste receptacle as Kliney nearly choked on his own tongue. "Nice touch, Klinedinst, the DEP said, his hand on the basket. He turned around slowly, looking at the work that had been done. "Good job," he added and left the cell. That was the last visit by a prison official for nearly a year.

It didn't take Botchie and Saint long to realize what a gem they had found in Kliney. Although neither of them understood why he'd risk a breakout since he didn't owe that many years, they didn't worry about it very much. In the meantime, their hopes soared even though they both knew there was an enormous amount of work left to do and they had no idea how much time it would take.

Kliney didn't seem to be in any great hurry. He didn't work every day and was totally committed to doing an absolutely thorough job. What he didn't want was some nasty problem raising its head halfway through the project. Neither did his partners. This was to be their way out and they wanted to do it right this time. In fact, both Botchie and Saint began to refer to Kliney's cell as the commutation room.

Now a little logistics problem arose, what to do with the spoils? Since the cell reconstruction was completed, they couldn't keep loading it on the trash truck. That would be too risky. Carrying the dirt out into the yard by the pocket full wouldn't work. Botchie had the idea to dump it in the yard. Kliney looked at him in amusement, shaking his head. "D'ya have any idea how much dirt we're talkin' about, Botchie?"

"Lots, but, hell, that's the way they do it in the movies."

Kliney shook his head. "We're gonna dig a hole about three feet on a side and a hundred feet long. That's over. . . " he screwed his eyes up and squinted in concentration, "Hell, that'd probably be enough loose dirt to fill up at least two cells clear to the ceiling, maybe three. We're not goin' to dump that on the goddamned basketball court and tamp it down with our feet, ya know."

Kliney finally decided they could flush the soil down the hopper into the sewer system. Unlike the earlier hoppers, those at Eastern did have a trap of sorts. So it wasn't a straight shot into the sewer. They'd simply drop the spoils, a little at a time, down the hopper. A short section of hose attached to the faucet above the hopper could be left running continuously to flush it out. This would work better than the normal flushing mechanism, which had a tendency to clatter each time it was used and annoy close neighbors. However, the slow water flow wouldn't carry away the small rocks that were dug up, so the spoils would now have to be screened.

The work was agonizingly slow at this point. Not only couldn't it be done on a daily basis, but it was just plain difficult working in the cramped space of the shaft. Things should go better once the horizontal tunnel work commenced. There was another problem in the form of the growing prison population. Kliney called a domino game to discuss the problems.

When the three men met at their usual place outside of 8 Block, Kliney started talking. "Look, if we can't figure a way to speed up this process, we're all goin' to be old greybeards b'fore we get outa here. An that ain't the only problem. I'm beginning to worry about getting a cell mate. If things get much more crowded, Martin's goin' to have to reconsider our deal."

Both Botchie and Saint nodded their heads in agreement and were quick to volunteer to dig themselves. And, of course, Kliney agreed readily.

"That'll help, but only one man can dig at a time and then for only half or three quarters of an hour. You have to close the door so you don't accidentally get caught and that's about how long it takes before ya run outa air. Pretty sticky business. What we need is a night shift. If I can pick my own cell mate, then I won't have ta worry about some damned stranger movin' in and he can work with me at night after lights out."

Once again, Botchie and Saint were in agreement. "Do ya have anybody in mind?" Botchie asked.

"Yeah, know a guy, name of Bill Russell. I've known Bill for a long while and he's got a lot of years to serve, probably jump at a chance to get outa here."

As it turned out, both Botchie and Saint knew Russell as well. He was a likeable fellow and not large–about 5' 8" and 145 pounds–which was an asset for a tunnel digger. Bill worked in one of the craft shops between 7 and 8 Blocks and was a master wood carver. Russell's masterpiece was a very large carving of an old western bar scene complete with cowboys, bar girls, and gamblers and with every minute detail including table, chairs, bottles and glasses. He'd been offered some good money for the piece, but wouldn't sell. Thought it was the best work he'd ever done. His meticulous nature probably equipped him well for the digging task. And aside from his craft skills, Russell would be able to provide critical materials they would eventually need.

Following standard procedure, Russell was invited to a game of dominoes. As Botchie and Saint listened, Klinedinst roughed out the plan. Russell's face was deadpan and his dark eyes darted from one man to another as he listened. Finally, Kliney put the question to him. "Bill, I need a cell mate I kin trust and we'd all like you to join us. This ain't a demand. If you don't want in, just say so, but we'd like ya to think about it."

This wasn't a decision to be taken lightly. The way Bill saw it was he could really escape and disappear into a new life; he might get caught and his sentence, already too long would become longer by at least ten years; or he might get shot to rag dolls. *Ah well*, he thought, *there's no way I'm gonna get outa this life alive anyway*. To Kliney he said, "Guess I've thought long enough. 'Preciate your confidence and the offer. I accept." The men shook hands all around and the bargain was made.

Kliney and Russell requested a meeting with DEP Martin which, of course, was granted. The next day, with Bill looking on, Kliney asked permission for Russell to move in with him. Mr. Martin looked a little surprised by the request since Kliney was a guy who's quiet as a fish and hoards his privacy. Kliney, sensing the DEPs thoughts said, "With all the people comin' in here, you're goin to be forced to double me up with somebody sooner or later. I'd rather choose my own cell mate, Sir." Permission was granted.

Now the work got serious. Botchie and Saint began putting their time in the shaft during yard out. One would dig and the other watch, trading off every forty-five minutes. With Russell there to watch, Kliney could pull an evening shift. With three men digging, the downward progress increased to at least 6 inches per day. Unfortunately they couldn't all dig every day, but every day the shaft got deeper. In a little over a month the men had reached the base of the foundation wall. They had finally reached grade. Now the digging would begin to count!

More time was needed in the tunnel and after lights out was the time to do it. The only problem was that the night guard made a body check on each cell every 30 minutes. At least that's what he was supposed to do. Since the guard neither suspected nor expected any problem, and the prison wasn't at high alert, the exercise was perfunctory. Just the same, the men couldn't afford to take any chances. Haste wasn't the objective. Freedom was. The work simply had to be interrupted every 20 to 25 minutes so there would be two men in bed when the guard arrived.

Kliney announced that it was time to go back to the domino board. "Look," he explained when everyone had gathered, "right now I can only work 20 or 25 minutes at a time after lights out.

Bill watches and alerts me when the guard starts his rounds. We need to have a 'dummy' to stay in bed all night, either in mine or Bill's. To do it, we need a plaster cast of a face and a hand."

Everyone nodded, but none were certain of what they were agreeing to. Kliney continued. "Bob McKnight works for the dentist and can get some of the plaster used to make dental molds. If you guys agree, we need to recruit Bob." All agreed.

McKnight was serving life for murdering a professional football player who was alienating the affection of his girlfriend. Bob accepted the offer with enthusiasm. Pilfering some plaster of paris for the head and hand casts was his first assignment. In addition, he started working in the tunnel during the afternoon shift. They weren't into the tunnel very far at this time so the extra hands meant that everybody could spend a little more time involved in their normal routine–both work and play.

And nobody had to work in the dark anymore. An extension cord was rigged using #12 weatherproof electrical wire. It was plugged into the light socket located over the desk mentioned earlier. The wire was concealed by a shirt hanging from the light fixture over the desk. Eventually the entire tunnel would be lighted by bulbs placed at intervals and attached to the tunnel's roof.

Things were going well and excavation of the tunnel proper had progressed around 10 feet when the work came to an abrupt halt. Kliney had done a terrific job of installing the tunnel cover and the fit was nearly air tight. Removing it was like pulling a cork from a champagne bottle–pop! One day as the cover was being removed there was strange noise, like PLOP, from inside the tunnel. Upon investigation Kliney found the roof of the tunnel had partially collapsed. The cover had fit so well that, when opened, it formed a partial vacuum inside the tunnel. Time for another domino game.

When the team had gathered, Kliney explained what had happened. Russell and McKnight expressed serious concerns, suggesting that prison was suffocating enough without getting buried alive in a tunnel beneath it. Botchie suggested drilling a hole in the cover panel to relieve the pressure. Kliney nixed that idea, explaining that the hole might be discovered. He proposed building a cribbing such as used in mine shafts to prevent cave-ins.

The cave-in and subsequent shoring cost nearly a month and a half of digging. The biggest problem was rounding up the material, primarily lumber. No place was sacred, the wood came from packing cases at the shop, crates from the kitchen, benches stolen from cells. When the material was all gathered, Kliney was the only person who knew how to do the work. This was no problem to Kliney, who seemed to relish the task. In fact, his teammates began to get the feeling that he was more interested in the engineering feat than the escape. Finally, however, Kliney notified all the guys that the digging could proceed.

Aside from Russell, who was often in the cell while Kliney was doing his work and went into the tunnel regularly, Botchie and Saint were the first to see the finished job. They looked in both amazement and admiration. "Damn, you do good work," Botchie said. Saint nodded in agreement and Kliney beamed. The tunnel was perfectly safe. The digging could begin again.

At this point, a sixth team member was recruited. Botchie and Saint talked to Kliney about inviting Horace (Bow Wow) Bowers, a friend of Botchie's, to join and Kliney agreed. Nobody thought it was necessary to do anything more than tell Russell and McKnight what they were going to do. There was no problem anyway; everyone seemed to think it was a good idea. Bowers was serving a life sentence for killing a Pennsylvania State Trooper. He was an extremely powerful man with the physique of a longtime body builder. Based on his reputation as a killer and a demonstrated willingness to take down anyone, Bow Wow was probably one of the most feared men at Eastern. As important, because of his crime the chance of the man ever being released was slim to none. He would have a vested interest in the success of the enterprise.

The digging was going very well. A full crew meant men could trade off making a full day's work possible. The plaster casts, arranged on either Kliney's or Russell's bed, allowed the night shift to labor in the tunnel without fear of discovery. Things were going very well for the conspirators. And then, calamity!

Chapter 11

Moving Up the Ladder

In August, 1944, a guard was killed on 9 Block.[1] The body was found in a utility room by guards arriving at shift change. Coagulated blood splatters covered the floor and walls, the result of multiple stab wounds. Bill Russell was busy flushing dirt down the hopper when he heard the news flash over the cell radio. "Murder at Eastern State Penitentiary, located on Fairmount Avenue in Philadelphia . . . a search for the killer or killers is underway . . . the State Police have been called . . . ." Russell's head snapped up as he heard the words. He knew what would happen soon. He immediately called down into the tunnel. "Kliney, Kliney!"

"Yeah," came the reply.

"You better get outa there right now. Double fast."

Kliney didn't waste any time climbing out of the hole. The story tumbled out of Russell's mouth and both men hurried to dump the remaining dirt back into the hole, replace the the door panel, and wipe down the cell floor. Both men were muttering and cursing as they worked. They knew this was a dangerous situation. The cops would tear the prison apart looking for weapons, blood-stained clothes and other evidence. This could be the end.

The expected shakedown came soon enough. The law was out in force–prison guards, state police and even the canine corps. They scoured every cell and building in the prison.   At each block the inmates stood naked in the middle of the block. While the guards watched the inmates, the State Police methodically tossed every cell. Beds were torn apart, desks searched, and foot lockers upended.

Joe Corvi had been in his cell carding pins when the horde of searchers arrived. He stood fully exposed like everyone else as 8 Block was ransacked. One of the block officers came by, one who knew Joe. "I hope you're clean, Joe," the officer said.

Joe grinned at him. "I'm clean as a whistle, Captain. As you can see."

At 7 Block the search began at the end closest to the rotunda and worked down toward cell 68. All of the tunnel team held their breath as the search commenced toward the end. Kliney and Russell had a lot of time to think about it.

Finally they arrived. Two troopers entered the commutation cell. Kliney and Russell, and probably everyone else, held their breath. Wonder of wonders, the two troopers, perhaps growing tired looked around, rummaged in the two chests full of personal goods, stirred up some papers in the "waste basket" and left. Whew! The prison lock down lasted for two full days. Inmates were fed in their cells by the guards. Nobody went anywhere and, of course, the tunnel stopped dead. Not a shovel full of dirt moved for three full weeks until everything calmed down.

A similar crisis occurred in December when somebody delivered a three-stick package of dynamite into the prison by throwing it over the wall. A mass escape plot was suspected and the warden ordered the prison locked down and searched. All cells, the exercise yards, and prison shops were combed for weapons, fuses, and blasting caps.[2]

The guard's killer was never identified and nothing came of the suspected mass breakout. Never-the-less, the prison came to red alert in both cases and tensions were high. The tunnel crew saw their chance for freedom evaporate. For Kliney and Russell, discovery meant not only the end of the dream, but time in solitary and extended sentences. Like breaching, attempted breaching is a punishable offense. However, all's well that ends well. When the dust cleared after the murder episode the mole men returned to their digging project. Although they were shaken by the search, they remained doggedly determined. Joe Corvi, on the other hand, was moving into a new job, a promotion in the prison administration hierarchy.

———

Corvi was on his way to Soup Alley, between 4 and 5 Block, to get a cup of coffee one morning. Deputy Warden Martin, Ole Stoneface, was standing in the center, arms crossed over his chest, watching what was going on. Or maybe he was waiting. When Joe approached, Martin waylaid him. Mr. Martin, of course, knew all about Joe's clerking experience at Graterford.

"Joe," the Deputy Warden said, "I'd like you to set up an office for Fred Banks, the new Vocational Director. There's space down on 10 Block alley near the Library."

"I assume you also want me to clerk for him?"

"That's right."

"What's it pay, Mr. Martin?"

"Six bucks a month I guess."

Joe was taken aback. The sum mentioned was far less than he was earning in the pin business. "But, Sir, I'm making $40 per month distributing pins. I want to help, but I need the money for my wife and kid." That, of course, was nonsense. Esther was earning very good money as a manager and buyer in an exclusive woman's shop. However, Mr. Martin didn't know that. Besides, why take a pay cut if it could be avoided?

"Don't worry about it, Joe," the DEP replied, "you'll be taken care of."

Joe took the job and started immediately scrounging a couple of desks, filing cabinets and chairs. Joe and Mr. Banks would occupy a "suite" of offices. There was a waiting room/reception area where Joe would work and two private rooms—one for Banks and one left empty. Corvi obviously was no interior decorator. Banks' office was sparsely furnished with a desk and a chair for the Director plus a second chair for a visitor. Joe's office contained a small desk and chair, a couple of filing cabinets and six straight back chairs for the waiting area. The walls displayed no adornment.

In no time at all Joe and his new boss were in business. The business involved interviewing all inmates entering the prison system and making recommendations regarding which institution the new arrivals should be sent to. Of course, this was nonsense. They were most often sent to the institution with room to spare. The Vocational Director was also responsible for job placement and job changes. Misconduct hearings were also a responsibility. Banks had to deal with questions of work history.

Banks, an American Indian, started in the penal system as a guard and eventually was promoted to Lieutenant grade. By the time he was promoted to Vocational Director he was 60 years old. Everyone thought Banks was a decent man and he was respected by inmates and guards alike. A thoughtful, soft-spoken man, he always had time to visit with a person. He had one monumental deficiency, though. Four years of schooling at an Indian Reservation school was the extent of Banks' education. As a result, Joe Corvi did almost all of the work in the office–interviewed all incoming inmates, recorded vocational histories, arranged for job transfers, wrote all the reports, and did all the typing. About all Mr. Banks had to do was attend staff meetings, and Joe even prepared him for that.

One of the more onerous responsibilities of the office was making up the monthly payroll. For Eastern, with over 1,000 inmates, this involved nine sheets of 8" x 14" paper, that's nine originals with eight carbon copies each. All those copies required a fairly heavy hand on the keys. The report was typed and could have zero errors and no erasures. This demand for perfection and the sheer volume of work involved caused Joe to put in some long hours at the end of each month. He was allowed to stay at the office as late as necessary and provided with a late snack as well.

The compensation issue Joe was initially worried about wasn't an issue at all. Every Monday morning Joe would find five packs of king-sized cigarettes in his bottom desk drawer, courtesy of Fred Banks. Smokes, of course, were the coin of the realm in prison–you could smoke them, wager with them or spend them for goods and services. In addition, Mr. Martin and Mr. Banks turned a blind eye on Joe's extracurricular activities, especially those involving the pin business. Working out of his office in the Banks' Suite, Joe maintained his $40 per month distribution business. In addition, he also cornered what, in prison terms, was a lucrative carding business. Newly arrived inmates, all of whom Joe interviewed upon arrival, were housed in 14 Block while being evaluated. These men were recruited to do the carding while they locked on 14 Block. The work was done in the spare office and the men were paid in conversation, candy and cigarettes, of which Joe had an abundance. Joe grossed about $86 dollars per month, with candy money the only out of pocket cost.

While Corvi spent his days in relative comfort and drew top wages for a prison economy, the tunnel crew toiled in the damp, dimly lighted, cramped passageway. It was muddy, the air was bad, and the work was hard. Of course, the mole men really were working for a different prize and measured their compensation in terms of inches excavated.

Chapter 12

A Hole at the End of the tunnel

At the twenty-foot mark, the diggers ran into a welcome obstacle–a large, old brick sewer line. Fortunately, the line was very close to floor level and required only a slight detour to get over. Kliney "borrowed" a sledgehammer from the maintenance shop and began working on the structure. The benefits were immediately apparent. The men had been sifting the spoils and disposing of them in the hopper. On top of the danger of exposing the project, it was also time consuming. Every shovel full of dirt was carried the length of the growing tunnel in various containers to reach the hopper. There were enough men to make it work, but it was tedious. One would dig, one would feed the hopper and the others formed a sort of bucket brigade to shuttle the dirt. Now, though, if they could penetrate the sewer line they had a better disposal alternative.

The men took turns beating on the brick sewer, which was about four feet in diameter, but it was difficult working because of the size of the tunnel. A full, powerful swing was impossible, but not any worse than hammering through the stone wall at the beginning of the shaft. However, just as the lyrics said in that old favorite, *High Hopes,* "... He [the ram] kept buttin' the dam," they finally succeeded in penetrating the sewer's wall. Bowers was operating the hammer when breakthrough finally occurred. The stench that erupted into the tunnel sent him into a paroxysm of retching and vomiting that left him weak and teary-eyed.

Later on, several of the men went into the tunnel and finished opening up the sewer. They initially had the same experience as Bowers, but finally got the hole opened sufficiently that they could see inside. What they saw made up for wretched odor they'd been forced to endure. A fairly good current carried the contents of the sewer along. From now on they would dump all the spoils, including the rocks, into the sewer. This would speed things up considerably.

———————

The Lord giveth and the Lord taketh away! No sooner did the team get into full production than another potential disaster arose. Inmates, like many other people, are creatures of habit. In a bar full of service men, the Marines gather in one spot, the Army gather in another, and Navy guys in still a third. In a prison yard, the same type segregation scheme is found. The blacks stay to themselves and the men from each cell block mostly hang out in their own area. This being the case, there was considerable consternation when a small group representing the New York mob and led by Willie Sutton, the notorious bank robber, invaded the space of 7 Block. The tunnel team was alarmed enough that they suspended operations pending some sort of resolution.

Willie and the gang invaded 7 Block's space during yard out every day for nearly three weeks. Botchie and Saint speculated that since the maintenance garage was in their area, the New York mob was expecting some sort of contraband shipment. Finally, the team met to discuss the issue.

"Hell," said Saint, "everybody from our cell block has noticed those bastards hanging around. So have the guards by now."

"Yeah," Botchie added, "those guys are up to somethin' and I wish I knew what."

Bowers was standing there taking it all in. As was his habit when standing around, he had his fists tucked under his biceps to make them look larger. "Screw 'em," he said, "I'm for running the bastards off." He grinned maliciously. "Let's me an Botchie an Saint go have a little talk with 'em."

So it was agreed and on the following Friday, while the prison staff members had their weekly meeting, the three men went to the office of the staff psychiatrist, where Sutton worked. Willie looked up, a hint of fear washing over his face, as the three inmates filed into the office, the last man shutting the door behind him. The trio casually surrounded him. Anyone confronted by three guys with such a reputation for violence would have been understandably nervous, but Willie was really in a state.

Bowers opened the ball. "What'r you and your girl friends doin' hanging around our area, Willie? Lookin' for trouble?"

"Jees, jees no, guys," Willie sputtered. "We didn't think anything of it."

"You didn't think period, ya little fuck! Now, you goin' to explain this or not?"

Bowers leaned on Sutton's desk, towering over him menacingly. "Well?" he shouted.

Sutton jerked in alarm. The story came in a rush. "Little Georgy, the guy I lock with, got to questioning me about surgically removing fingerprints and stuff like cosmetic surgery. This kid is in for 30 to 60 so I figured something was going on. I also knew he was a friend of Bill Russell and figured that Russell was up to something. We're just fishing around. Hell, I'm in for life myself."

Willie stopped and looked at his interrogators imploringly. "No kidding guys, that's all there is to it."

"Okay, Willie. We believe you," Bowers half snarled. "But we don't want to see any of youse guys hanging around our turf again. Understand?"

Willie sat there, sweat beading up on his forehead.

Saint paused at the door after Bowers and Botchie had left the room. He turned back to Sutton. "Not a word about this to nobody, understand. Not one word. If anything happens, we might let you know."

Later on the team had a meeting and was told about the confrontation with Sutton, including Russell's possible complicity. Russell, after some beating around the bush, admitted he had told someone that there were plans. No specifics revealed, just plans. The guy's name is Georgy, he added with a little prodding.

The same three guys who had braced Sutton went to visit with Georgy. They found him in the yard behind 9 Block and maneuvered him into a corner. The kid was visibly shaken as Saint nailed him with his glittering black eyes. "Hear you're interested in cosmetic surgery, Georgy Porgy. We'll be happy to 'commodate ya. A little ear surgery, ya know. Maybe remove a bit of yer nose. As for the finger prints, I kin take care of that too." Saint paused a moment and stuck his nose in Georgy's face. "I'll cut yer goddamned hand off."

Georgy shook like a leaf and his pants darkened at the crotch. The three men turned abruptly and walked away, leaving him standing in a puddle of his own urine. A short time later Georgy got a transfer to Graterford.

Now the tunneling resumed at a pace. Soil was moving day and night and there were always at least two men at work. The group decided to bring in another guy to help. Vic Symanski was a young guy, only 25 years old, but was serving 20 to 40 years for armed robbery.[1] He was a ferret of a man whose size made him perfect for packing spoils back to the sewer. Including Vic meant his cell partner, David Aikens, would also have to be brought into the group. There were now eleven men involved.

So much material was being moved that the sewer was beginning to get clogged, primarily because of the rocks and small stones being dumped. Botchie and Saint volunteered to clear the line. Both took a deep breath and went in somewhat gingerly. The smell was still horrendous, but because they were working in it every day, they didn't notice it as much. However, this was different. Now they were going to wade in the filth. And, if that weren't enough, they soon discovered that they had company.

Scores of huge, brown sewer rats scurried through the sewage. The invasion by the humans threw them into a fever pitch of activity. Rats squealed and scuttled everywhere, racing frantically all over the bodies of the two men. Botchie and Saint were using short lengths of boards trying to shove the solids away from the opening. Just a trickle of raw sewage began to run more freely. Saint began screaming hysterically, and flailed every which way with his digging board. Botchie took a couple of solid licks before Saint threw the board away and hurtled himself out of the black hole.

He lay on the floor of the tunnel writhing in a fit of panic. For once Botchie had no comic lines to utter. Never had he seen Saint in fear of anything, but he certainly was terrified of rats, and these were big rats.

After Saint calmed down a little, he began talking very rapidly. "Goddamn, I can't stand those slimy, filthy bastards." He shuddered reflexively and hugged himself. "Botch, I'll never be able ta come down here again."

"Don't worry 'bout it, pal. You'll only have ta get in the tunnel one more time and that's when we leave this place." And that's the way it happened.

In February they hit the outside wall. So close! Everyone took a turn at seeing and feeling the stone wall. Now they had to dig four and a half feet down through rocks, chunks of mortar and other debris left behind by the stone masons who built the place over a hundred years earlier. It was tough digging, perhaps the toughest of the entire project. And the wall's base was incredibly thick, maybe fifteen feet. And then another problem bubbled up–water in the tunnel!

The tunnel was dug on a slope to get under the wall. One night Kliney, who undoubtedly spent more time than anybody on the job, was excavating the down slope under the wall. He hit an underground spring that began leaking a little water and then a little more. For a few days, the men, disheartened, took turns watching the water level. The thought of digging for nearly a year only to be stopped at this point was more than any of them could bear.[2] However, the water level, even though it didn't recede, didn't get any deeper either.

Finally the digging started up again. Directly under the wall, at the lowest section of the tunnel, the water was about 16 inches deep. It was spooky working in those conditions. The men tried making a little dam to hold the flow down. No matter how hard they tried they still had to scoop mud and water every day, with little more than head room between the water's surface and the roof of the tunnel. Production was sometimes no more than an inch or two a day.[3] There was really no way to measure accurately. Finally, after nearly a month of extremely hard labor, they made it to the far side of the wall. Freedom was only a few feet above them.

The tunnel continued on an upward slope in order to reduce the risk of a cave-in, and the digging became progressively easier. Finally, on the third day after clearing the wall, signs of grass roots could be seen. That evening the word spread among members of the tunnel team, "Tomorrow's the day, we're leavin' this place."

On the morning of April 3, 1945, after a year of hard labor, the men entered the tunnel for the last time. For Sutton, who was invited along after all, it was the first time. They all left their cells late for breakfast and, one-by-one, slipped into cell 68 in 7 Block, climbed down the ladder and started crawling the 100 feet to freedom. Nobody spoke. All that could be heard was their breathing as they scurried through the tunnel.

———

An ice wagon driver named Daniel Flowers was passing the prison at Fairmount and 22nd Street around seven o'clock. He watched in amazement as men began to pop up out of the ground right next to the guard tower. "They popped out like so many brown rats," he said. "I couldn't count them, they came so fast, but they dropped off over the wall [the low wall just outside the 30 foot prison walls] the moment they came out and scattered down side streets in all directions."[4]

Flowers continued. "I was scared to death," he said, "but some of them ran right past me and didn't even look at me. They were covered with mud from head to foot." The ice man guessed that the whole bunch got out of the hole in three minutes flat. The last man to emerge, Willie Sutton, sprinted west down Fairmount Avenue.

———

Sutton, the last man in and the last out, was also the first to be captured. At the same moment that Patrolman John Hamm rounded the corner at 22nd and Fairmount, Sutton had the extreme bad fortune to pop up out of the hole in the ground and sprint up the street for all he was worth. Hamm gave chase and was joined by another officer, George Hummell. Both chased the convict firing their revolvers. They finally caught up with Sutton at 24th and Fairmount. Sutton gave up without resistence.[5]

By the end of the day, five more of the escapees were back in prison: Bowers hijacked a milk truck and along with Mickey Webb, Bob McKnight and James Simister led the police a merry chase around Fairmount Park until they were rammed by a police car. Bowers attempted to escape even then, attacking a policeman with a shiv, and was shot for his trouble. All four men were taken into custody and returned to the prison before nightfall. About two hours after the breakout Kliney was spotted by two patrolmen near 11th Street and Huntingdon, about a mile from the prison. He was recaptured after a brief chase.[6]

Bill Russell walked into a trap on April 10 while attempting to visit an old girlfriend in Frankford, in northeast Philadelphia. Turns out the girl's father was a policeman and had laid the trap on the day of the escape. When Russell arrived at the girl's apartment dressed up like a sailor and ready for courting, he was met by a squad of Philadelphia's finest. By that evening, Russell was in the prison hospital being treated for seven gunshot wounds.[7]

Aikens and Szymanski where caught on the same day in a wooded area near Wawa, Pennsylvania, about 17 miles northwest of Philadelphia.[8] All this time, James Grace had been hiding under a bridge in Fairmount Park. Worried about what would happen when he was caught, he simply walked up to the front gate of Eastern at about 5:15 A. M., April 11, knocked on the pedestrian door and surrendered. The story is that the guard initially told Grace to go away and return when the prison was open for business.[9] By the end of the day on April 11 the only men still at large were James Botchie Van Sant and Frederick Saint Tenuto.

Chapter 13

Freedom Is Fleeing

Like everyone else, Botchie and Tenuto, number two and three out of the tunnel (Kliney was number one), hit the street a muddy mess and took off on foot. They soon concluded that safety was not in numbers and went their separate ways. Botchie managed to steal some clean clothes off a clothes line. Then he joined a trolley full of commuters in Fairmount Park, rode it to Manayunk, where he made himself as small and inconspicuous as possible. Two men driving to work apparently failed to notice that the hitchhiker looked like he'd just emerged from a primordial swamp and gave Saint a ride in the back of a truck. He was dropped off near the Naval Yard. From their respective hidey holes the two escapees nervously awaited their ride.

Eventually Toadie Hines, a friend of Botchie and a former inmate at Eastern, picked up both men. It was after dark when they arrived at the Buckeye Club, on 8th Street in South Philadelphia. The club, located on the second floor, was called a weekend club because it was open to the public only on weekends and so it was empty on Tuesday, April 3. On the third floor, above the club, there was a small efficiency apartment with access up the back stairs located in the club's storeroom. This was their safe haven, at least for several days. There was plenty of liquor behind the bar and, of course, there was a pantry full of food in the apartment as well as some fresh clothes. Toadie had been busy since Botchie's initial contact a week earlier.

Botchie managed a phone call to Toadie when the crew finally made it under the wall and had started the upward drift to freedom. The ex-con was warned of a "happening of some note" and was told he'd be contacted. He knew what the happening was when the radio broadcasts announcing an escape began earlier that day.

It had been a harrowing day for Botchie and Tenuto, in fact one of several harrowing days. First there was the long sleepless night preceding the escape and then the general scramble and confusion following the "coming out" party. The waiting around during the day was probably the worst of it. Both men expected the cops to show up at any moment. Now they were safe, or relatively so. Saint grabbed some beers as Toadie led his two companions through the club and upstairs. After cleaning up, which felt incredibly good, and wolfing down some food, the men returned to the bar for some serious drinking and talking.

Tenuto looked around. "Ya know, this is right where I did Jimmy DeCaro." He got up and looked carefully at the hardwood floor in front of the bar. "Maybe there's a little blood stain right here. This's where he fell. Floor looks a little darker."

All three men looked and nodded. Then they turned their attention to the whiskey bottles arrayed on the back bar and started talking. It was nice to relax and have some drinks. The tension was shed like the winter coat on a stray dog.

"You guys been in the news all day ya know. Six of ya was caught already."

"Who," Botchie asked.

"Don't know for sure, but one of 'em was that Sutton guy." Toadie paused, thinking. "Oh yeah, your pal Bowers was shot, Botchie. It was quite a chase. Bowers an some guys stole a milk truck or somethin'. I'll get a paper in the mornin' an you kin read all about it."

Botchie chuckled. "I'll bet ole Bozo Smith's having a cow right now. His pen's sorta sprung a leak." Now Botchie was laughing uproariously. It was a tension release and an expression of pure pleasure and a song of victory. They'd beaten the man!

Tenuto grinned lopsidedly. "You'll think cow, if he ever gets holt of ya. Shit, they'll be piping ya sunshine."

Eventually the conversation turned to how the men were going to get out of Philadelphia and where, exactly, they were going. "We got to get outa here. There's no place to hide for long with the cops turning up the heat. Hell, they'll have every snitch in the city looking for us," Saint said.

Botchie was thoughtful. "It's only Tuesday. We could hole up in the apartment while things cool off. Toadie, can you get us some decent clothes, some cash to tide us over and some hardware?"

"Yeah, jus need a couple a days. I'll get right on it." Toadie's face brightened, "Say, you know Mike Quinn?" Without waiting for an answer, Toadie continued. "Lot a heat on him around here. He an a bunch of guys robbed the Casa Blanca Roadhouse down near the Garden State Park race track a couple of months ago. There was some killins. Some guys was murdered after the Roadhouse job.[1] Heard he was hangin' out over in New York."

"Sure would be handy if we knew where Mike was. Can ya find out, Toadie?" Botchie asked.

"I'll ask around, somebody might know."

———————

It took only a few days to round up all the material requested–money, suits and an arsenal of fire power. Toadie also had some news about Quinn that he shared with his "house guests".

"Ya know, looking up Mike Quinn might not be such a good idea. Course, that's just my opinion." Toadie paused to see if he had everyone's attention. "The grapevine has it that he's been doing jobs in New Jersey, Pennsylvania and New York an the Feds are hot on his trail. Right now he's holed up on the West Side in New York. I'm trying to get a better line right now."

"Kin you get us to New York?" Botchie asked.

"Yeah, I kin get ya a driver. The problem is gettin' ya across the river inta Jersey. There's still road blocks all over the place in eastern Pennsylvania."

"We'll think about it. You got any idears Saint?"

Saint had been thinking. "How bout we get shipped outa Philly as freight. Ya know, along with a truck load of produce or somethin'. Have yer guy pick us up with a car someplace in Jersey."

"Good idear. we kin do that," Toadie replied. "When ya wana go?"

Bill Russell made up their minds for them. The next day Toadie brought in a newspaper that described, in detail, the capture of Bill Russell. The Philadelphia police had shot him all to rag dolls and the newspaper account said they were about to pronounce him dead until the coroner arrived and found that Russell was in pretty bad shape, but still alive. Russell was under guard at the hospital and still hanging on.

The problem was that Russell knew about the Toadie connection, including a phone number. Bill was a solid guy, but who knows what a man will say when he's all doped up as he surely would be. Both Botchie and Saint agreed that they'd better be on their way, so Toadie worked out the details. They would go to Trenton in a van packed with a load of furniture. A guy by the name of Jack Morino would take all their gear and pick them up there for the trip to New York.

Chapter 14

The Aftermath

At 7:00 A.M. on April 3, 1945, Joe and several hundred other inmates were at first mess. The men ate breakfast with minimum chatter and returned to their cells as required. What was different was second mess wasn't served that day and neither was lunch or supper. The jungle drums started beating almost immediately with news rippling down the cell blocks, moving from cell to cell. "There's been a breakout! Maybe two dozen guys bailed out." Within an hour the news flashes began:

Convicts escape through a 99-foot tunnel under the wall of Eastern State Penitentiary . . . The escape was staged just after 6:20 A. M. At that time 317 men, part of the prison's population of 964, were removed from Cell Blocks 7, 8, 9, and 11 and taken to breakfast. . . .[1]

City detectives report it was a wholesale break plot with at least 22 convicts taking part . . . twelve convicts got away . . . five were caught by prison guards as they crawled out of the tunnel. Five more were trapped inside the tunnel.[2]

At 7 A. M. "Slick Willie" Sutton, reportedly the last man out of the tunnel, surrendered to police officers John Hamm and George Hummell after a brief chase. Sutton, a four-time offender serving a life sentence is believed to have engineered the tunnel break. . . .[3]

When Joe heard the bit about Sutton being the mastermind behind the break, he snorted in derision. Like many in the inmate population, Corvi had little use for the pint-sized blabber mouth who was always singing his own praises. "Hell, he [Sutton] couldn't lead a blind man from one side a the street to the other," Joe said. Years later Joe's friend Botchie would tell him, "Sutton didn't know 'bout that hole til the day he crawled through it."

Joe's next thought was *Cheez and crackers, here we go again.* He was thinking about the killing and the suspected escape attempt of the previous year. All the prisoners had been locked down for three days with only a sandwich on the evening of the first day. Now the men were locked down again and a first head count had already been taken. There would probably be a couple more before the authorities would be satisfied that everyone was accounted for.

By the end of day one, April 3, Joe and everybody else knew about the tunnel that started in Kliney's cell on 7-Block, that 12 men had escaped and that six, including that notorious bank robber and escape artist, Willie Sutton, were back in custody. Kliney, Webb, McKnight and Simister, along with Sutton, were locked up in the segregation block–1-Block. Bowers was under guard in the prison hospital with a gun shot wound. Six guys were still out. *Good for them*, Joe thought.

———————

On the day of the break out, Bozo Smith, the warden, was obligated to make a report to the State Secretary of Welfare, Miss Sophie M. R. O'Hara. In turn, she ordered the Director of Corrections, Fred Brady, and two prison inspectors to make a thorough investigation into all the details and circumstances that may have led to the break. The investigation, which took about a week to complete, apparently discovered no unusual circumstances leading to the breakout,[4] other than the fact that a number of inmates had spent an entire year tunneling out of the prison right under the noses of the cell block guards and Deputy Wardens who were responsible for inspecting the entire prison twice daily.

In addition, there was a Grand Jury inquiry. When the members of the Grand Jury visited the prison, they were met by Warden Smith, who politely answered their many questions. One of the jurors, in fact, did ask, a bit sarcastically, how a tunnel had remained undetected for such a long period of time. The question was the answer to Warden Smith's prayer. He smiled benignly and responded in a low, steady voice.

"This penitentiary has more than thirteen hundred cells. In addition, there are shops, a hospital, garages and all manner of facilities necessary to the workings of the institution." He paused to let this information sink in. "And, there must be miles of maintenance tunnels running under the cell blocks. Gentlemen, since I became warden, in 1928,[5] we've had inmates attempt goin' over the walls, through the gates and about thirty tunneling attempts–none successful until now. As to your question, I know exactly which cell the tunnel begins in, and I'm goin' to give you the benefit of that knowledge. Let's see if you can find the tunnel."

The Warden then led the Grand Jury members from the central control area down 7-Block to the end, stopping in front of cell #68. Standing beside the cell door, Smith said, "This is the cell the tunnel originated from. Please go in and see what you can see."

Kliney's cell had been put back in order, just like he was still living there. The Jury members filed into the cell and looked around. They moved the bed away from the wall. They moved the desk and the foot locker. They even tried to move the hopper and peered carefully into the wastebasket attached to the wall next to the cell door. The jury members looked perplexed. One member went so far as to comment, with not a little impatience, "Come now, Warden, there's no tunnel in this room. Take us to the proper cell."

Warden Smith must have been relieved. At any rate he gloried in the moment, smiling   solicitously. Then, with a magician's flair, he removed the wall panel hiding the tunnel's entrance and stepped back remarking, "Mr. Klinedinst, one of the prisoners who occupied this cell, was a real artist, wasn't he? Here's the tunnel entrance, hidden in plain sight, so to speak."[6]

The lockdown ended on the fourth day when the normal routine was reinstated. Joe was working in Banks' office when he got the news of Aiken and Szymanski being captured somewhere out near Wawa[7], Pennsylvania. Russell was shot up four days later while trying to visit his girlfriend.[8] At about 5 A. M. The following day James Grace crawled out from under a bridge in Fairmount Park, walked up to the prison and surrendered.[9]

Weeks passed and Botchie and Saint were still at large. For Joe Corvi, the invariable routine of prison life continued. The calendar counted the days until his release. The war in Europe ended in early May and Japan was on the ropes. The men who survived the fighting would be coming home, starting all over again.

Joe wondered about the year-long effort of the escapees and the risks and worry associated with the tunnel project. Twice during the year, when the guard was killed last summer and during the dynamite episode in December, the prison had been on high alert, significantly increasing the possibility of exposure. Less than a week before the escape, Kliney's cell had been tossed when an escape rumor was circulated. All of this must have been nerve wracking for all the men involved in the escape plot, most of whom were now serving time in isolation.

Cheez and crackers, now comes the trial. They've all added at least 10 years to their sentences. Maybe Tenuto and Botchie will make it. Doubtful. Hell, escape attempts alone must account for 25 or 30 years of their sentences. I'd never even think about breaking out–the risk is enormous and the potential penalty astronomical!

Chapter 15

The Last Men at Large

Botchie and Saint, hidden in a truckload of furniture, made it from Philadelphia to Trenton on the main road, Route 1, without a hitch. The truck was stopped briefly at the toll bridge over the Delaware River and the driver questioned. The two men sitting amidst the load could only worry and sweat when the truck stopped. They had no clue about what was happening. When the truck drove on after a few minutes delay Botchie and Saint both heaved a sigh of relief. At Trenton, they were picked up by Jack Morino and continued the trip to New York by car.

It was raining and dark when the men arrived in New York. Quinn was waiting for them as planned.[1] The luggage was loaded into Mike's Packard and they were on their way within minutes. In about 30 minutes the Packard pulled into an alley off Amsterdam Avenue, stopping in back of a three-story apartment house. They climbed the back stairs up to the third floor and Mike let them into a small but comfortable apartment.

"This is home guys," Mike announced with wave of his hand. "There's groceries and beer. Make yourselves at home. I and a friend of mine got some business to attend to. When I get back we'll see what we can set up for you."

"Jees, Mike," Botchie said. "This's a nice place. Really 'preciate your help."

"Think nothing of it, pal, you'd do the same for me."

That night Quinn and his friend, Joe McCann, drove down to Camden, New Jersey, cruised around for a while and finally pulled up on a deserted street and parked. "That's the place right over there," Mike said while pointing at a brick row house three door down the street on the left.

"DeSanctis is supposed to be living there now, with a sister I think. The cops turned him loose a few days ago."

Joe mumbled something and scrunched down in his seat, making himself comfortable. Mike lit up a cigarette and waited. At about 5:30 a milkman came by, stopped and dropped off milk at several doorways. There were no lights on in the buildings, so Mike left the car and walked down the street. At the closest apartment he stopped and looked around. Then he walked up to the front stoop, took a bottle of milk and casually returned to the car. He and Joe shared the milk, which was still chilled, and continued watching.

At about 8 o'clock people were moving about and kids were heading to school. Still no sign of life at the apartment they were watching. Finally, a short, heavy set man came out of the door and stood on the stoop for a moment, looking around. He didn't notice the car with the two men in it up the street. The man was dressed casually–open throated white shirt, a vest and baggy trousers. "That's him," Mike Quinn announced.

As the man began walking down the street, Mike started the car and slowly followed. McCann pulled a .38 pistol out of his waist band. Mike had a .44 single action revolver. The car stopped and both men jumped out just as the man they were stalking walked past an alley between two buildings. McCann and Quinn started firing almost simultaneously. The man, Romeo DeSanctis, jerked spasmodically and clutched his chest before falling into the alley. He was dead before he hit the ground. Quinn and McCann piled back into the Packard and sped off. Later, a neighbor who had stuck his head out of a window to see what all the noise was about, would identify the two killers and the Packard for the police. He even recalled the license number and that the car

carried New York plates.   The dead man, DeSanctis, was a key
State's witness in the Casablanca Roadhouse robbery.[2]

Back at the Amsterdam Avenue apartment, Botchie and
Tenuto were sitting in the living room having a beer and reading a
day old newspaper. It was late afternoon when Mike knocked on
the door. Saint picked up a .38 revolver and stood back as Botchie
asked in a low voice, "Who is it?" When Mike responded, Botchie
opened the door admitting both Quinn and McCann.

"Hey," Mike said with a grin. "You guys making it okay?"

"Goin' out of my mind, cooped up in this place," Saint shot
back.

"We can fix that easy enough. Anybody hungry?" Mike
paused, as if for a response of some sort. "Know a great restaurant
right around the corner." As an after thought, he added, "This is
Joe McCann. Joe, meet Botchie VanSant and Freddie Tenuto."

The men shook hands and Joe said, "So youse guys is the
famous mole-men, hey. Mike's told me all about ya." He half
giggled, half cackled at his own humor.

Tenuto looked sharply at Quinn. "Relax, kid, Joe's okay.
We do business together."

Looking at Botchie, Quinn said, "We got some stuff to talk
about. I imagine you guys need some cash. Let's talk about it over
dinner and drinks. Okay?"

It was a small, neighborhood restaurant.   The sign
announced Griffin's Bar and Grill. There were a few early diners,
but otherwise the four men had the place to themselves. They
chose a table at the rear of the dining room and ordered drinks from
a waiter who wore a white shirt with a bow tie and had a soiled
white apron tied around his waste. Mike called the man by name,
Frank, and exchanged pleasantries. He'd been there before. The
table companions were a study in contrast. Mike wore a slick
looking double breasted suit–dressed to the nines–while McCann
had on a wrinkled open-necked shirt and slacks that needed a
cleaning and pressing. Tenuto wore the trousers from a suit, white

shirt and a vest. Botchie looked more like a factory worker just starting off the week with a fresh set of clothes.

After the drinks had been delivered, Mike started talking. "We've got a bank job planned up in Long Island City. Me and Joe'll go inside. Need a driver and a lookout. It'll be a four-way split. You guys interested?"

Tenuto replied instantly, "Yeah, I'm in."

Botchie thought about it for a minute. *I just got out of the House and I sure don't wanna go right back in. Oh hell, we do need the cash.* To Quinn, Botchie nodded his head affirmatively.

On Tuesday, April 15, Mike Quinn quickly walked up behind the bank manager just as he was opening the front door of the bank. He put a gun to his head, said something in a low voice, and walked the man right into the bank with Joe following close behind. Joe's job was to corral the other employees as they arrived and keep them covered with a shotgun. Mike escorted the manager to the vault and sweet talked him into opening it with the help of his .44 revolver. Botchie lounged at the corner of the building, looking inconspicuous, and Tenuto sat behind the wheel of a stolen Studebaker with the engine running.

Business was going well inside the bank, but not outside. Botchie noticed a car pull up and park. Four men in the car watched the bank. Botchie strode to the door, rapped sharply three times, and kept right on going to the car. Mike and Joe boiling of the bank like bees leaving a nest, and the four men in the car piled out. Joe emptied the shotgun, gave it a toss, pulled his pistol out and kept on shooting. He immediately drew fire and was hit several times. Mike was hit in the leg as he jumped into the car just as it pulled away. Tenuto hit the throttle and took evasive action as he headed out toward Shea Stadium where the Packard was parked. They switched cars and, with Mike laying in the backseat groaning, the men then skipped over to Queens Boulevard and wandered, at a leisurely pace, back to the Amsterdam apartment. It was a wonder, but they had gotten away. They found out later that Joe was killed and the men chasing them were feds.[3]

The robbery had been a total bust. Not only was Joe killed but the   take was small on account of the inside team leaving early. The question of how come the cops showed up in the first place remained a puzzle. The bottom line was they needed a big score rather quickly and they needed to leave New York City. First the score and then the exit.

———————

After returning to the apartment, Tenuto was dropped off and Botchie took Quinn to a friendly doctor who patched him up. Later that same afternoon found the bank robbers sitting around the apartment, licking their wounds and discussing the future.

"How in hell did the FBI find out about the job?" Quinn muttered, almost to himself.

Botchie looked at his friend, who had his right leg propped up for comfort. "Doesn't matter. They did. Question is what do we do?"

"We get out of town, that's what we do. First we get some money, then we get out of town," Saint said.

"Well, I can't go back to my apartment now," Mike added. "If the feds knew about the bank job, they probably know where I'm stayin'. 'Fraid I'm goin' to have to stay with you guys." There was a pause as Mike thought. "Look, we've got a couple of banks to choose from. One is the National City. I'll arrange for a car and a driver. You guys go look the place over . . . you know, when they open, when people arrive, cop patrols. I'll join you as soon as I can get around a little easier. In the meantime I'll get a friend of mine to help me pick up some of my stuff."

Tenuto's face couldn't be read. He looked like a sphinx. Botchie thought: *This stinks, but I'm snookered. Don't feel good bout this at all.* On the other hand, he knew that there was little choice. They had to have a stake in order to leave and if they didn't leave they'd in all likelihood be caught. It was one of those 'damned if you do and damned if you don't' situations.

The men took their time 'casing' the bank, in an attempt to insure success. A friend of Quinn's, an ex-convict himself, drove his own car. The men took turns walking around and inside the bank over a period of several days. And, one or two at a time they'd just sit in the car and watch the traffic for any regularities such as frequency of police patrols and presence of traffic cops. Finally the men set a date for the hold up–it would be Tuesday, May 22nd.

Philadelphia Captain of Detectives Joseph Kearns got a call on Wednesday, May 16, from New York detective John Nothels. Kearns scribbled some words on a yellow legal pad: VanSant and Tenuto believed holed up–Broadway and 130th Street area–maybe Amsterdam Av.-apt–Nothels. If this lead was accurate, it could mean the end of the manhunt for the last two holdouts of the April 3 prison escape. If Quinn was with them, as expected, so much the better. Kearns called for detectives David Litvin and Bill McGowan, two of his veterans that had been assigned to the case.

When the two men arrived, Kearns briefed them on the news from New York. "I want you guys to go to New York and hook up with John Nothels. He'll be your liaison and will provide all the help you need. How do you want to do this?"

It was Litvin who answered. "Don't know if Bill agrees or not, Joe, but I think it'd be a good idea to let Doyle and Henningsen take the lead. All three of the guys we're after have been in an out of here several times. One of 'em might make us, but not the young guys."

And so it was agreed. All four of the men would travel to New York, but Dick Doyle and Mike Henningson would make up the surveillance team and set up housekeeping in the neighborhood. The men drove to the city that night and met with John Nothels. John arranged for both men to stay at a boarding house on 130th Street just west of Amsterdam. Tenuto had been seen in a local taproom which, it turned out, was two doors down from the fugitives' apartment on Amsterdam Avenue. Late the following morning the two Philadelphia detectives walked into Hennessy's Taproom and ordered a beer.

Both the detectives were dressed like working men, rough clothes and work boots. They immediately made themselves at home in the taproom–drinking beer and playing shuffleboard with the locals. By Saturday, when there was a shuffleboard tournament it was like the two detectives had always been around. Mike Henningson beat the local champion and drank beer on the house the entire evening.

All the time they were playing, the Philadelphia cops were also working, taking turns watching the apartment doorway and the street for any sign of the fugitives. Finally, on Sunday evening Tenuto actually came into the taproom and bought three quarts of beer. He left immediately, followed by Henningson who watched Saint enter the apartment house. Now the law knew exactly where the bad guys were, but not if they were all together.[4]   Saint returned on Monday evening, had a draft at the bar and carried another three or four quarts back to the apartment with him. By now the neighborhood was discreetly but well covered by the New York police and the two other officers from Philly. All that was required was the right moves, and that happened on Tuesday evening.

———————

Saint carefully closed the apartment door behind him and stood on the stoop at the top of the stairs, looking around with feigned casualness. Satisfied that all was well, he descended the stairs and, thrusting his hands into his trouser pockets, walked briskly down Amsterdam to 130th Street, turned right to Broadway and then up Broadway to Griffin's Bar and Grill. He waved at the bartender and joined another man at a table toward the rear of the room. The man already at the table was Mike Quinn, who had left the apartment ten minutes earlier. He was in shirt sleeves, but wearing a tie. A navy-blue, double-breasted suit coat was draped over the back of his chair. Mike grinned at Saint and asked, "You feeling a little better." Saint merely shot him a stony glare. Monday evening Tenuto had gotten thoroughly sloshed and sick, in that order. The plan had been to do the bank and leave New York on Tuesday morning. Now, on account of Saint, it would have to wait until tomorrow.

The bartender, unbidden, brought a second draft beer, placing it in front of Saint. "Where's your buddy today," he inquired. He was just attempting to be friendly but failed miserably. Both men ignored him. Tenuto gazed into the foamy head like it was a crystal ball. It was getting late in May and beginning to warm up in the city. Right now he was smiling to himself. It had been nearly two months since the escape. All they had to do was make it through tomorrow and out of the city and they'd have it made.

When Botchie left the apartment, a short distance behind Tenuto, Doyle and Henningsen followed separately, but signaled Nothels to call in the cavalry–their quarry would soon all be in the same place. Nothels called the station and six patrol cars were immediately dispatched to the scene.

Within a few minutes Van Sant joined his companions at the table. After a third beer had been delivered, the men began to talk quietly about the delayed bank robbery. Tenuto was clearly embarrassed and simply listened. After a brief discussion, apparently satisfied that all was in readiness, they turned their attention to the menus. Neither Botchie nor Saint were yet accustomed to the novelty of choosing a supper of their own liking instead of look alike, taste alike, smell alike prison fare.

The three men were so engrossed in making their selections that they failed to notice Doyle and Henningsen enter the restaurant. The two detectives walked right up to the table. Suddenly, weapons materialized and Doyle said, "Stick 'em up; we've got you." Three heads snapped up in unison, a look of fright and confusion on their faces.

Quinn was looking directly down the business end of semiautomatic pistols in the hands of two men who looked like construction workers. Then he saw the badge one of the detectives was holding up. "You got us," Quinn exclaimed wildly, as he threw his hands up. "Don't shoot." Although all three of the men were armed with revolvers, they wisely kept their hands in plain view. No sense arguing with drawn guns pointed at you at close range.

Quinn, who was on parole from Pennsylvania, had been at large for some time for several armed robberies and murders. Saint and Botchie, of course, had been absent without leave since the tunnel escape less than two months earlier. The captives were removed to the Detective headquarters on Center Street and interrogated until the wee hours. All three naturally denied involvement in any crime while staying in New York, and none could be identified from the Long Island City robbery. Also, they only carried two or three hundred dollars on their person. The police concluded a robbery was planned, but planning isn't a crime. They were arraigned early Wednesday and all three waived extradition. Before the morning was up, the men, under close guard and in separate cars, were on their way back to Philadelphia.[5]

Chapter 16

The Crime of Prison Breaching

As soon as Tenuto and Van Sant arrived back at Eastern, the entire gang was loaded up in a sheriff's van and taken to the courthouse to stand trial before Judge Harold S. McDevitt or "Hanging Harry," as he was affectionately known to the inmates. The inmates filed into the courtroom under heavy guard and were seated in two rows of six men each. This non-jury trial was to be by the letters, rather than by the numbers. Judge McDevitt started with 'A' and that meant Dave Aikens.

"David Aikens, you are charged with the crime of prison breaching. How do you plead?"

Aikens was dressed in his prison clothes, like all the men. He looked drawn and haggard and every one of his 58 years. He replied, "Not guilty, Your Honor."

Exasperated, the Judge snapped, "How can you plead not guilty when you were caught in Wawa, a town located 30 miles from the penitentiary?"

"If Your Honor would allow, I'll explain."

His honor sighed. "Proceed."

Well, Sir, our cells at The House ain't got no hot water. Everybody's gotta go ta the shower room clear at the end of the cell block ta get hot water for washing eatin' pans and utensils and such. I generally get my water just b'fore mealtime, and, it being early morning, I was still a little groggy. There was two lines, one went to the shower and the other, it turns out, went into Kliney's cell. I got in the wrong line. First thing I know I'm crawlin' inta a hole in the wall and just naturally commenced following the rear end of the guy ahead a me. When I got outa the hole, I figured nobody'd believe my story anyway. And, since I'm not guilty of the crime I was servin' time for, I figured I just take off and prove my innocence."

Judge McDevitt failed to see the humor in Aiken's story. He didn't crack even a glimmer of a smile. After a very brief pause he banged his gavel down and shouted, "Guilty as charged. I sentence you to ten to twenty years." He punctuated his words with another bang of the gavel and said, "Next."

James Grace was the next up for justice. "How to you plead?" asked the judge.

"Not guilty, Sir."

"Okay, what's your story?"

"Your Honor, I'm not guilty of prison breach. However, I am guilty of leavin' the scene of a crime."

"Explain, Mr. Grace," the judge demanded.

"Well, Sir, the way that prison's operated is a crime. So, it seems to me that what I done was leave the scene of a crime."

Still no inkling of a smile. "Guilty as charged. Ten to twenty years."

By now everyone was persuaded that they were all going to get the maximum sentence regardless. That being the case, they'd just as well have a little fun in the process. Of course, nobody was guilty. The excuses ranged from "I missed my girlfriend awful bad." to "The devil made me do it." Sutton's attempts to impress the Judge with his vast legal expertise failed. His reward was ten to twenty years. Saying something amusing might have gotten him a lighter sentenced. Botchie claimed ignorance, explaining that he thought breaching meant breaking and he didn't break anything. "I just crawled out of an existing hole, Your Honor." He got ten to twenty years as well. Kliney, who engineered the whole project, only received a three to six year sentence. Perhaps the judge thought Kliney was duped and that Sutton really was the ringleader. Bowers and McKnight were tried for hijacking the milk truck and received 15 to 30 years each.[1]

———————

All twelve of the men who took part in the tunnel break expected that after the trial they would be placed back into the general population. Bad assumption. They grossly underestimated Warden Herbert E. Smith's rage. The breakout was a personal affront, an assault on his reputation and, although he may only have suspected, would ultimately cost him his job.[2] The man had a reputation for being tough, but fair. Fair went out the window with what he considered betrayal. Every man was sent back to the 1 Block, the segregation block. One hour per day of yard out, short rations and absolute isolation from the general population. Not quite sensory deprivation, but pretty close. Neither was this to be a short term situation.

Although interaction with inmates outside segregation was extremely limited, the tunnel gang, for all their shortcomings, were emotionally strong and creative. They had each other and the radio and books. One of their favorite pastimes was listening to the radio game show, Twenty Questions. In this show, the host had a certain person, place or thing in mind and a volunteer from the audience was allowed twenty questions to unravel the mystery. However, the tunnel gang enjoyed more playing their own game. The men took turns playing host and volunteer, shouting questions and answers through the wicket in their cell doors. The game often continued for up to two hours.

Some of the gang also participated in spelling bees among themselves, using Mike Quinn, the best educated among them, as the spelling master. Aside from the games, which could go on for hours, there was reading, physical exercise and writing letters, that is assuming there was somebody to write to.

Some of the guys, who were nearly functionally illiterate, found letter writing all but impossible, but they tried anyway. Most of the inmates had been incarcerated for years and had never written to anyone. This was a new and frustrating experience. When they sat down to write, they were ambushed by their lack of language and the silent stutter of getting started. For direction they turned to Quinn.

Jimmy Grace, the 24-year old serving 12 1/2 to 45 years for armed robbery, approached Quinn one day. "Mike, I need ta write ta my girl friend. I mean, I wanna write, but don't know what ta write or how."

Quinn waited for the kid to go on, but he didn't. "So? What do you want me to do?"

"Well, I thought, maybe, you being smart an all, that you might, like, write it for me."

"I don't write letters to other people's girl friends, Jimmy. Don't recite poetry to them either. I'll help you though."

"But I don't know how."

Quinn thought for a moment. "If your girl was standing right here, this minute, what would you say to her?"

"I'd tell her how much I missed her."

"No, no. What, exactly would you say?"

Probly I'd say somethin' like, "Jees, Ginny, I sure miss ya a lot."

"And then?"

"Been a long time since I seen ya."

"Jimmy, if that's what you'd say, then that's what you should write. Try it and we'll see what we can do with it."

Jimmy tried it and it took hours for him to write. Mike Quinn coached but didn't write a word, only offered some corrections. This was the process he used to help his friends. This is Grace's letter to his girl.

Dear Ginny,

I sure miss you lots. Been a long time since we seen each other. Guess I screwed up pretty bad on that last job when they sent me to the house. Tried to get out an it was in the papers. A big bust. Never even thought about being captured. Just did it. Now I don't know how many years I got to do. Lots. Don't know if I'll ever see you again.

                              Your friend,
                              Jimmy

All of the guys dealt with segregation differently–some fought it, some accepted it, and some assumed the fetal position. It was Botchie, with his irrepressible sense of humor, that consistently lifted the spirits of his friends. He was the self-appointed jailhouse poet–also said to be a poor one–but the best locked on 1 Block at least. He remembered the headline of a newspaper article that was captioned *The Leaking Pen* and decided to compose a poem of the same name. He'd work on those verses every night, maybe only completing a stanza or two. The next day, through the wicket, he'd recite his most recent efforts to all the inmates on the cell block who cared to listen. His friends seemed to get a kick out of his work, so Botchie worked his poem until it was completed.

Somewhere, nobody seems to know, there's an epic that Botchie left for posterity and shared with his friend Joe Corvi years later. It's said to be more than a hundred stanzas long. Of course, he had a lot of time on his hands. Here are a few sample verses:

THE LEAKING PEN[3]

We're here in segregation.
Our lives the worse they've been,
The fault of Smith's damnation,
Cause we sprung a leak in his pen.

Twas Kliney's notion to dig the hole,
For our early commutation.
We burrowed round like a bunch of moles.
The result bein agitation.

Sutton claims he done it all,
Which is just as well I guess.
He'll do the time, the Judge's call,
And we'll all be in for less.

After a time the men became dispirited and fell into fits of depression. The months piled on each other until they'd been in segregation for seven months. Even Botchie's normally high spirits were considerably dampened. The usual chatter and games were absent. The men all understood they should be punished for their action, the system had awarded most of them an extra 10 to 20 years. "What more did they [the authorities] want anyway, to turn us into a bunch of nut cases?" They asked that question often when they conversed in the yard.

The answer to that question may have had something to do with Warden Smith's damnation, as suggested in Botchie's poem, but it probably had more to do with one Cornelious J. Burke, the new acting Warden. Smith was ignominiously removed from his position, the direct result of the April 3 breakout. Smith probably would have relented and returned the tunnel gang back to the general population in time. Burke was a different story altogether. He never forgot a slight, a betrayal or a transgression. Once crossed, he never forgot and would be relentlessly venomous and vengeful. The new warden was the deputy warden at Graterford when Botchie and Saint went over the wall. When Botchie was in the hospital, after being captured, Burke came to visit. Looking down, his eyes implacable dark pools of rage, he said, "Van Sant, you will regret this day for the rest of your life." Apparently he meant it and had Botchie right where he wanted him. The rest could stay in segregation to keep him company.

None of the inmates realized what sort of man held them in his power. All they knew was that something needed to be done. What they decided on was a hunger strike to draw attention to their plight. On October 8, all but Bill Russell began their fast. All breakfast trays delivered to their cells were returned untouched, the same for lunch and supper. Day after day the strike continued with the striking inmates accepting only water.

On October 17, the ninth day of the strike, the media was leaked news of the strike by a sympathetic guard, Big John Sweeney. An Inquirer headline on that day read "11 Convicts Refuse to Eat at Pen: Enter Ninth Day of their Hunger Strike, Officials won't Interfere." Acting Warden Burke was quoted: "The convicts are on a hunger strike in protest against being kept in solitary confinement . . . They want to mingle with the other prisoners, perhaps to plot another escape.[4"]

On the tenth day of the strike, prison staff doctors examined the striking inmates. Urine tests indicated that the majority of them were cheating. They weren't living high off the hog, mostly cookies and candy purchased by sympathetic inmates from the commissary and smuggled in to them, but they were eating. Only Botchie, Saint, Bowers, Webb and Kliney had held firm. Several days later Warden Burke capitulated, probably more from fear of the media storm that would accompany the death of an inmate from starvation than consideration for their health. The men were removed from their cells one at a time for a conference with Deputy Warden Frank Martin. Martin told each of them that if they would end the strike, their grievances would be given serious consideration, That night, a voice vote was taken through the wicket and Martin's offer was accepted.

Shortly afterwards five of the original dozen inmates were transferred to Holmesburg County Prison–Saint, Willie Sutton, Dave Aikens, Spence Walden and Kliney. Of course, the remaining seven were all wondering what would happen to them. Botchie was taking bets that they wouldn't return him to Graterford. On Thanksgiving, a nice gesture, Mickey Webb, Jimmy Grace and Bill Russell were released into the prison proper. During the Christmas season, another nice gesture, James Semester and Bob McKnight were also released into the general population. In March 1947, Horace Bowers also left 1 Block, leaving Botchie the sole occupant in segregation of the original twelve escapees. He recalled Warden Burkes' ominous threat about regretting his escape attempt, "You'll regret this until the day you die."

Chapter 17

The Notorious Holmesburg Prison

Beffore Tenuto and the other five transferees were sent to Holmesburg the authorities there were given ample alert and advised to prepare maximum security quarters for the newcomers. The officers there probably laughed. Holmesburg was opened for business late in 1896 and to date there had never been a successful escape. However, just to be on the safe side, certain steps were taken. The men from Eastern State would be locked in the punishment block, probably forever, so the security was already excellent. The walls were eighteen inches thick. The door frames were constructed of inch thick cast iron. Bolted to the framework were steel doors made of two-inch straps. For added security a solid steel door was welded to the frame work.

The layout at Holmesburg was exactly like Eastern State with the wheel and spoke design, but only seven blocks radiated out from the hub. The doors between the hub and the cell blocks were solid steel with a peep-hole rather than a barred door. No guard entered the cell block with a key to the front door on his person. A second guard waiting at the front door locked and unlocked the door from the hub side.

Security on the block was tight. The inmates locked there were completely isolated from the rest of the population. They never left the block except in the case of a medical emergency. Meals were brought on a food truck and served by a kitchen employee who was constantly observed by a cell block guard. During the night a cell check was made every 30 minutes with the same entry and exit routine by the guards as described above. Once a day two inmates at a time were allowed out into a small exercise yard surrounded by a fifteen-foot security fence. In other words, men housed in the insolation block were locked down tight.

When the transferees finally arrived they were each briefed by Dr. Frederick Baldi, who wasn't the Warden, but appeared to be in charge.[1] The good doctor made it abundantly clear that the new "guests" weren't welcome and none were trusted any farther than he could throw them.   Each man was given the same stern admonition to behave himself: "You were ordered to this institution by Harrisburg. Otherwise you'd never have gotten through the front gate. If you cause trouble here, any trouble at all, the consequences will be extremely severe. This penitentiary has been here for half a century and there's never been an escape. If any of you try anything, your heads will be blown off." Baldi really worked himself into a froth and the message was crystal clear–this wasn't going to be any picnic.

After the lecture, each man was accompanied by two guards to the punishment block. When it was Spence Walden's turn, the guards opened the door for him and closed it. Then one of them, for some reason, ordered Spence to push the door open. He pushed on the door to no avail. The guards voice rose in volume and Spence pushed harder, as hard as he could. There was a sharp snapping noise and the entire door fell into the cell block. The guards leaped back and Spence, horrified, screamed, "I didn't do anything, I didn't do anything."

The guards immediately leaped on poor Spence and disabled him. Then, while one guard held the prisoner down, the other examined the door. What the guard found was that the weld had broken. They found out the hard way that steel can't be welded to cast iron and if it is, the weld fails under slight pressure. Spence apparently applied enough. All of the doors had to be rehung and bolted to the frame.

Saint, who had been a guest at Holmesburg years earlier, as had Joe Corvi, Sutton and anybody else arrested and held for trial in Philadelphia, knew that all of the keys in the prison were kept in a secured key locker located in the central control area. Saint, however, possessed another piece of very significant information. There was a 40-foot extension ladder chained to the wall at the powerhouse and the key for the ladder lock was also kept in the key locker. These circumstances offered some intriguing possibilities, and the next time Spence Walden and Saint were in the yard together they talked about them.

"Spence, there's a locker in the hub where all the keys are locked up. All of em. An I know there's a 40-foot extension ladder locked in the power house."

Saint had his friend's complete attention. "So how do we get the keys an the ladder?"

"Ain't sure yet. Wanted to see if there was anybody interested first."

"Well, I'm interested. What's next?"

It was agreed that Spence would be sick the following day so that somebody else could yard out with Saint. Turned out that was Dave Aiken, who proclaimed himself in. On the next exercise period Spence went out with Sutton. When Sutton heard a plot was in the making he was first alarmed and second incredulous. "What, are you guys nuts or something? Knowing about locks and ladders is a stretch from gettin' out. I don't want anything to do with it!" At that, Sutton couldn't get away from Spence fast enough, which was a little tough in their small, private yard.

Finally, the remaining men decided that an attempt would be made if they could get a weapon of some sort. They also decided that Sutton was coming along whether he liked it or not.

Saint managed to get a message to a friend in the population with the help of the inmate who delivered the kitchen food cart to the cell block. The friend agreed to supply a shiv which would be delivered in the food cart during the supper break. On a day the menu included soup, the weapon would be in the soup kettle wrapped in a protective cover so it couldn't make any noise being delivered. The inmate who served supper was warned to ladle the "package" only when the guard was distracted and to deliver it to anybody but Sutton. After several attempts over as many weeks the shiv finally was delivered to Spence. Now they had to figure out a way to get out of the cell block and to the keys.

"Okay, this is the plan," Saint said to his partners, except Sutton. After he explained, he asked for approval or rejection. Each man agreed in turn that the plan was worth a try, although any rational man would have flatly rejected it as being far too risky. But, all four of these inmates were facing what amounted to life sentences, and were desperate to get out, regardless of the risks.

On February 10th it was snowing heavily, a storm that continued into the night. After lights out, during one of the regular cell checks, the guard found Saint huddled on the floor of his cell in a fetal position. He was moaning quietly and laying in what appeared to be a puddle of vomit (actually the well-chewed remains of his dinner, mixed with a little water). The guard rushed back to the cell block's front door. "Tenuto's really in trouble. Gotta get him some help. Gimme the key," he blurted out.

The guard, named Greenwood, hurried back to the cell and half helped-half hoisted Saint to his feet. The "sick" convict leaned heavily against the guard and shuffled along beside him, grasping his stomach as he moaned in agony. At the block door the outside guard unlocked and opened it. Then he witnessed a remarkable recovery. In a flash, Saint threw a choke hold on the block guard and held a glistening little shiv to his throat. "Get in here right now an close the door quiet like," the 'sick' inmate demanded.

The control center guard took one look at Saint's glittering black eyes and did as he was told. Holding his hostage, Saint made the second guard walk ahead of them back to his cell. Once there he locked them up and quickly released everyone but Sutton. Then they returned to Saint's cell and ordered the guards to strip down to their skivvies. The guards stripped off their clothes, all the time watching the shiv waving menacingly in their faces. Finally, they were both bound with some cord stashed for this moment and gagged with their own underwear.

On the way back to the cell block door, Willie was ordered out of his cell by Tenuto, who wore a guard's uniform, and left in the care of the other escapees while Saint hurried into the control area and the key locker. He easily found the keys he needed (they were all labeled) and hurried back to the cell block. The men made their way out the rear door of the block and let themselves outside into the storm. Three inmates walked ahead of the two officers to the wall of the powerhouse, unlocked the ladder and proceeded toward the wall. The falling snow concealed their movements as they crossed the yard, placed the ladder against the wall, and climbed up. Each hung full length and dropped, in turn, down the other side. The distance to the ground was at least six feet less than the inside height and all the men made it without mishap.

The escape succeeded in spite of the impossibility of it. It should never have happened and several guards were dismissed because of it. Willie Sutton, who was made an offer he couldn't refuse, later wrote that the only reason the escape worked was the improbability of it and a security system that had grown lax following over fifty years of success. He also claimed the escape was his idea and he was the leader.[2]

The next day Joe Corvi sat in his office at Eastern State reading the daily paper. The headlines leaped out at him: "Five Escape From Holmesburg." The article went on to say that three of the convicts were captured and returned to the prison within two hours. They were Spencer Walden, David Aiken, and Clarence Klinedinst, and the article described the checkered history of all three, including their escape from Eastern State Penitentiary almost three years earlier. Willie Sutton, the celebrated bank robber and escape artist and Frederick Tenuto, a veteran or four breakouts himself, were still at large. Sutton, the article said, was suspected of being the ring leader. "Cheez and crackers."

Willie Sutton, the reluctant escapee, went to ground in the New York area. Eventually he moved to Long Island where he worked at a convalescent home and moonlighted as a bank robber. Ultimately Willie left the rest home and moved in with Nora Mahoney, who lived in a small town close to his former employer. Willie continued to ply his trade and probably would have been caught sooner or later anyway, but fate interceded in the form of one Arnold Schuster who recognized Willie while both were riding the subway in New York and identified him for the police. When the judge was done with him, Sutton was sent to Attica State Prison in New York with a minimum sentence of 132 years.[3]

Saint was the subject of an intensive search and was featured on the FBI's most wanted list for years. He was never seen or heard from again, at least not by anyone who'll talk about it. But that's another story.

Chapter 18

Botchie's Story

Days passed into weeks, weeks into months, and months into years. World War II had ended, the Korean war had begun, Truman was president, and James Van Sant and Michael Quinn were still locked in segregation. Perhaps Warden Burke considered Quinn guilty because of his association with Botchie. Or, perhaps, he simply wasn't taking any chances. At any rate it was only the intercession of fate that finally got them both released.

One day, not long after Christmas 1953, an inmate locked several cells down and across the block from Botchie decided to register a fiery complaint. This was not a rational act, but one of anger and frustration–an emotional explosion. He set fire to his straw-filled mattress and commenced screaming for help. Botchie and everyone else on the block could clearly hear him. Apparently the man thought that a guard would come to put the fire out and the inmate would subsequently be taken before the Warden where he would register all his complaints–no mail, no visitors, no privileges, no nothing. Unfortunately, the inmate thought wrong.

An officer of the cell block came all right, striding toward the cell with determined steps, like an angry parent about to deal with a child throwing a tantrum. This guard didn't have much use for inmates and, in particular, this one. He neither looked into the cell nor asked what was wrong. In fact, he really didn't care. The guard slammed the wooden containment door shut. The closed door muffled the cries of the inmate. It also shut off any ventilation there was. Smoke filled the cell along with the trapped inmate's screams.

Little tendrils of smoke found their way through cracks in the cell door and soon became clearly visible to those inmates locked on the other side of the block, Botchie included. First, merely one inmate hollered the word 'fire'. Then the word rippled throughout the block until it crescendoed into the hoarse, panicky roar of fifty voices. The cell block guard came running. By now the smoke was streaming out of the closed cell. The foolish guard threw open the wooden door and fumbled with a key. Luckily there was no fire to flash with the sudden draft of air. Smoke poured out of the cell and spread throughout the block. Teary eyed inmates coughed and gasped for air.

Soon additional guards appeared, one with a fire extinguisher which was quickly directed at the smoldering mattress. Skylight vents were opened to clear the smoke. Two guards dragged the hapless arsonist, who had died of asphyxiation, out of his cell. An inmate in an adjoining cell heard the original guard say, "That'll be his last fire, by God." Now there would be hell to pay.

An investigation was ordered by the District Attorney's office. A young assistant District Attorney named Sam Dash was in charge. One afternoon shortly after the inmate's death, Botchie heard the sound of unfamiliar footsteps and voices. Botchie was standing at his cell door peering through the bars when the group finally appeared. There were several men dressed in civilian clothes and accompanied by Deputy Warden Martin. One of the men came to Botchie's cell and began to ask him questions about the inmate's death.

"I'm Sam Dash, the assistant DA, what's your name?"

"James Van Sant, Sir."

"I'd like to ask you some questions about the fire and the inmate that died."

"Pardon me, Sir, but, with all due respect, that guy's dead. What can you do for me?"

Dash stared at Botchie for a moment. He hadn't expected this turn of events. "What is it you want, James?"

"It'd be nice just to get out of solitary and back into the population."

"How long have you been here?" Dash inquired.

"It's been so long I think I was born here, Sir. Been over eight years and that's a record."

Dash, who appeared both sympathetic and keenly interested, kept asking questions until the whole story came out. Botchie told him about the events that landed him in 1 Block to begin with–the tunnel escape, the release of the other escapees years earlier, and the reason he thought he was still here. He ended his discourse with a final statement. "I screwed up, Mr. Dash, and sure deserved punishment. The court gave me ten years for the escape, Maybe a little time in solitary is okay, too. But being locked up, like a caged animal, for eight years is just too damned much, sir."

Dash was clearly upset by what he'd heard. "I'm inclined to agree with you, James, but there's nothing I, personally, can do. You need to present what's called a Writ of Habeas Corpus Ad Subjiciendum to the court. Basically, the writ will question the lawfulness of your long restraint in solitary." Dash then told Botchie how to prepare the document properly.

Botchie and Mike Quinn worked on the writ together, because there was no other help available. When the work was completed, they gave it to Big John Sweeney, the sympathetic block guard, to get mailed. It was returned with a note asking for a copy for Warden Burke. The men did as they were requested. The next day they were told the governor needed copy. This procedure continued until they'd rewritten the writ seven times. However, Botchie's and Quinn's persistence prevailed. The writ was finally submitted and a hearing date set.

Everyone on the block knew about the upcoming hearing. The two inmates had a lot of support, some from unexpected quarters. One day Big John came by Botchie's cell and flipped a folded piece of paper inside. The paper contained a short note of explanation and two dozen numbers. The numbers identified inmates who had suffered mental breakdowns while locking on 1 Block during the time that Botchie and Quinn had been locked in there. Some were transferred to the hospital block and treated by the Eastern State psychiatrists. If they responded, they were returned to solitary to complete their punishment time. Those that didn't were sent to the Farview Hospital for the Criminally Insane at Waymart, Pennsylvania. Farview was usually a one-way ticket.

D-1441	D-7558 (F)	D-8680 (F)	E-136	E-866
D-2211 (F)	D-7856	D-9087 (F)	E-230	E-1639 (F)
D-5231	D-7920 (F)	D-9426	E-457	E-2004
D-7144	D-8360	D-9571 (F)	E-470	E-2444
D-7395 (F)	D-8685	E-136		

The hearing of James Van Sant and Michael Quinn was held before Judge Raymond McNeille. Representing the DA's office was none other than Sam Dash. Dash, an early and vocal critic of inhumane prison conditions, provided the two inmates valuable support and assistance during the hearing. When the judge observed that he couldn't believe the two men had been held in segregation for over eight years without even a hearing, Dash said, "I didn't believe it either, Your Honor, but it is a fact. I checked." When Botchie was being questioned by the judge relating to inhumane treatment, it was Dash that excused himself and encouraged Botchie to present his 'list' to the judge.

"It's a list, Sir, of men who were serving time in the solitary block and went crazy as a result. Mental breakdown, or somethin', is what Big John Sweeney called it." The judge nodded and ordered a bailiff to bring him the list.

"Mr. Van Sant, these are all numbers."

"Yes, Sir, lots of men ain't got names in prison. They're called by number, hey you or just inmate."

Judge McNeille's jaw muscles were visibly twitching. "And what is the significance of the 'F', Mr. Van Sant?"

Those men were sent to Farview, the insane asylum, Sir. Once a man's sent there, he's done."

"Done? What do you mean, done?"

Botchie fidgeted in his chair, a bit uncomfortable with the questioning. "Well, Sir, it means he dies there. He's never released."

McNeille looked at Sam Dash questioningly. Dash nodded in agreement.

That hearing might not have been all legal and proper and the writ may not have been appropriate, but it didn't matter. Somehow or other, the media had packed the courtroom and the two inmates got a great deal of friendly press as a result. Very shortly thereafter, James Van Sant, Michael Quinn and Spence Walden, who had been returned to Eastern after his escape from Holmesburg, were all informed they were to be transferred to Western State Penitentiary in Pittsburgh.

Big John Sweeney came for the men one morning and, along with some other guards, escorted Botchie, Quinn and Spence to the hub. There, after a search, they signed for the little money they had in the prison account. It was time to leave. Each man was shackled to two very large state troopers and marched out to waiting automobiles–one prisoner and two troopers to each car. At the north Philadelphia train station, they had to wait for a while. When the train finally arrived they had to wait for it to unload. Botchie noted that some of the new arrivals were being greeted by friends and a few received hugs and kisses. Botchie looked over at Warden Burke, who had come to make sure they got safely away. The three inmates and six accompanying troopers were standing together when Botchie pointed at Burke and said in a fairly loud voice to nobody in particular: "If I have ta kiss that sour puss, I'm not goin'." Quinn and Spence got a good laugh out of the remark. The troopers stood stone-faced and simply ignored the entire scene. Not even the hint of a smile.

Their arrival at Western State Penitentiary was without anything more than the usual formalities. The men were placed in the prison population, which was great as far as they were concerned. Mike and Botchie were assigned to the bake shop and Spence went to work on outside maintenance. Aside from some extra normal surveillance, everything was just fine. Until one day. . . .

Nobody said a thing to them. They never even saw the block guards, let alone talked to them. One morning the three transfers from Eastern were not allowed to leave their cells for work. At about 9:00 A.M. several guards arrived and took the men, one at a time, to what was call Home Block at Western State Penitentiary–segregation, the home of the condemned and trouble makers. No explanations were given and a request for a personal interview with a DEP was ignored. All that was said was: "You are all under investigation."

After being locked on Home Block for a month, Botchie wrote to a friend named Charley White and asked him to get him an attorney. Two days later Botchie was brought before Warden Maroney.

"Have a seat, Van Sant," said the Warden, nodding to one of two chairs positioned in front of his desk.

Maroney held up a letter. "This letter to Mr. White won't be necessary. You and your friends are all going back into the population this morning."

"Yes, Sir," seemed a sufficient reply.

The Warden continued. "An informant told us that you three had plans to smuggle guns into the prison. We investigated that allegation and determined, finally, that is was without basis. However, given your reputations for escapes, I thought it prudent to lock you down while things were being sorted out."

Maroney seemed genuinely concerned and regretful that the time in segregation had been necessary. "I'm sorry that we had to do that to you and your friends." Then he took Botchie completely off guard. Maroney offered his hand and a firm grip, an incredible gesture for a warden, at least in Botchie's experience.

Botchie had been locked in Western State for two years when he was summoned to Warden Maroney's office. Getting right to the point, Maroney said, "Botchie, I have orders to send you back to Eastern State." That was it, no explanation. Botchie's heart sank. He was actually fearful of being back in the hands of Cornelius Burke and spending another eternity in segregation. But when he arrived in Philadelphia there was no Warden Burke there to greet him with a mean, glowering expression. Instead, he was actually greeted at the entrance by none other than Johnny Bowers and several other acquaintances. There was something wrong with this. *Burke would never allow this stuff to happen. These guys shouldn't be down here without some guards around.*

The welcome was brief. Soon he was on his way to the DEP's office and was greeted cordially by Colonel Martin. After a bit of small talk Martin said, "We got a new Warden, Botchie, William Banmiller from over at Graterford. Unfortunately, he couldn't be here today, but you have an appointment to meet with him in the morning. This man is totally different from any Warden I've ever worked with. You'll like the difference." Martin paused a moment while Botchie digested the news. He heaved a visible sigh of relief. Martin smiled. "You were a little worried, weren't ya. Guess I kin understand that. You should know that Banmiller is the guy who got you transferred back here."

"Why would he do that?" Botchie blurted out.

"I'm sure he'll tell ya all about it in the morning." Martin was grinning, like he had a private joke. "You'll be lockin' back on 7 Block with your old friend Johnny Bowers" The Deputy Warden stood up signaling the end of the interview. "I'm sure you can find your own way to cell 56, you can go there now."

Botchie left Martin's office in a daze. *If Corvi was around there'd be a whole box of cheez and crackers. This is very strange. You kin find your own way. Be damned!*

At breakfast the next morning, the reception from many of the inmates was unbelievable. Botchie was greeted warmly by men he hadn't seen in ten or twelve years. Botchie told Joe Corvi about it when he saw him later on that day. "Guys were callin' out greetings left and right. It was 'Hi, Botch' and 'Good to see ya, Botch.' I was half way expectin' a bunch of roses from somebody. I tell ya, Joe, I was crying like a baby."

After breakfast, back at the cell with Bow Wow, Botchie paced. The cell, unaccountably, seemed very small. The work lines were called at eight o'clock and still no word from the Warden. *Guess he doesn't come to work til nine, another hour.* Bow Wow left for work. "Take it easy, Botchie. Ever thin'll be okay."

As soon as the work lines cleared, the block officer came by the cell and told Botchie to go to the front gate. He walked about half the length of 7 Block towards the back door. *Don't get any hopes up, dummy. Yer luck's been running downhill all yer life.* He got to the end of the cell block, went out the door and turned left toward the gate. The big gate opened as Botchie approached. He appeared calm, but inside he was shaking like a leaf. One guard beckoned him inside and another led him up the stairs to the Warden's office.

———

William Banmiller was a slightly built man with a warm, friendly smile. He was soft spoken, didn't assume aggressive postures and opted for civilian clothes rather than the traditional black or navy blue uniform. In short, he appeared to be the antithesis of the typical warden found in the eastern Pennsylvania penal system to date. When Botchie entered his office, Banmiller rose from behind his desk and walked around to meet the inmate and shake his hand with a firm grip. "Botchie," the Warden said, "I think it's about time we met." Banmiller thanked the guard for bringing Botchie up to the office and then dismissed him politely. He asked his visitor to have a seat, beckoning to a chair in front of the desk.

This behavior was totally foreign and Botchie was taken aback. In fact, he was speechless–partly because of the extraordinary behavior and partly because of the man. The two men looked at each other for a moment before the Warden began speaking. He laid his hand on a thick file lying on his desk. "I have your file here and have studied it carefully. The record is a puzzle. On the one hand you have robbed people, shot people and escaped from prison–how many times?" The Warden smiled in a friendly manner. "It's no wonder my predecessor considered you, ah, troublesome." He paused. "On the other hand, while in prison you have never abused anyone and were never physically violent. To the contrary, you have helped a good many younger men who were locked on 1 Block by using yourself as an example of what can be expected from continued deviant behavior. True, you were always attempting to 'breach the walls,' so to speak, but I guess you thought that was your God-given duty. Mr. Sweeney, before he passed away, told me that during those many years in solitary you never lost your sense of humor and your spirit was never broken. "And," he added with a chuckle, "he shared some of your poetry with me."

Botchie, nearing 50 years now and with 20 of those years in prison, was a skeptic. He didn't know what to think and was having difficulty believing what he was hearing. It was clear this man was thoroughly familiar with his record, but wasn't troubled by it. Equally clear was the fact that Banmiller didn't view him as a number. He seemed genuinely interested. Then the Warden's voice interrupted his thoughts.

". . . your escape attempts not withstanding, Botchie, I see other qualities that seem to indicate that you are rehabilitated. I think we should apply for commutation."

Botchie's head snapped up. He was dumbstruck, incredulous. "Pardon . . . pardon me, Sir. What did you say?"

"I was saying I think it's time you were released. You should apply for a commutation.
It may take more than one attempt, but I think we can manage it."

"Mr. Banmiller, I don' know what ta say. All my life I've only wanted ta be free and have only dug myself a deeper hole. Now yer sayin' I can be free–just like that. I can't hardly believe the Warden of this prison, of all people, took the time ta help me."

Banmiller smiled warmly. "Believe it Botchie. Now, the first step is for you to get an attorney to represent you in Harrisburg."

———

The first thing Botchie did after leaving the warden's office was look up Joe Corvi. He knew Corvi had gone the commutation route and wanted to know who he used as an attorney. Besides, maybe Joe could tell him a little about the warden, his guardian angel.

The office of the Vocational Director was empty except for Joe. He smiled broadly at the sight of Botchie and jumped up from his desk to shake his hand. "I knew you were back, saw you at mess this morning. How're you doing?" Joe was slapping his unexpected visitor on the back and Botchie was just grinning.

"Doin good, Joe. Doin better than good." Corvi would be the first to hear the news. "Damned if I'm not on top of the world. Mr. Banmiller jus told me to get busy on a commutation. I need an lawyer and thought you could help."

"Well, cheez and crackers," exclaimed Joe as he embraced Botchie. "That's terrific news. Good for you!" Joe backed off and just looked at Botchie who in turn looked embarrassed. "Sure, I know just the lawyer, the guy I'm using. He's a crackerjack on commutations. Named Morton Witkin, I'll give you his address."

After Joe looked up the address and telephone number, he wrote both down. Then the men talked for a little while, with Botchie describing his time at Western and how he came to be transferred back to The House. "Mr. Martin told me that the Warden done it. Couldn't believe it!"

"Banmiller's quite a guy, Botchie. For one thing, he's sympathetic toward the inmates and there's a good reason for it." Joe stopped a moment to gather his thoughts. "His Dad, Bill Sr., was some kind of bank executive who got his hands in the till. Did time at Graterford. Young Bill would come visit as often as allowed an those visits took place in the Warden's office. At the time, the warden was Mr. Leitheiser and he took a liking to Bill. When the old man was released, Bill was hired as the Warden's secretary. When Leitheiser retired he was replaced by Charles G. Day and Bill continued working for Day for several years. During those years working for the wardens, Bill earned a law degree from Temple University.

"One of the Deputy Wardens quit over a prisoner's strike and Banmiller was offered the job. Said he'd take it on two conditions: One, He wouldn't wear a uniform except on formal occasions. Two, he would pass judgement on inmates if necessary and award appropriate punishment, but he wouldn't do the deputy line. He wouldn't stand for the daily misconduct hearings. His conditions, amazingly, were accepted. He held that position until the Parole Officer job came open.

"Part of that job was to represent inmates who couldn't afford a lawyer before the Commutation Board. Finally, he was appointed Warden here at The House. He's sure different, probably cause his dad was a con. When he first arrived here, I had to provide him the files on every inmate housed here. He knows everyone of em by name. Goes out in the yard all the time, without the usual escort, and takes time to talk to the guys.

"One time I was out in the yard with some of the guys, Johnny O'Brien, Henry Sabey and a couple of others I don't remember. So, here comes the warden, dressed in his suit and wearing a soft felt hat. When he gets close, Sabey grabbed his hat, shoved his fist into the crown and threw it on the ground. Banmiller's just a little guy, you know, but what heart! He looks at Sabey for a moment, kind of sad, picked up his hat, straightened it out, dusted it off, put it back on his head and leaves. Not a word was said about the incident. That was anybody but Banmiller, Sabey, at best, would have rotted in the hole. If it'd been somebody like Burke, he'd a been a dead man. Me an the other guys just left Sabey standing there alone. Never had anything more to do with him."

Joe finally stopped and grinned at Botchie. "Guess I told you a little more than you wanted or needed, hey?"

Botchie just shook his head. "Never woulda believed a guy like that would be a warden, let alone give me all that help. Ya know, Joe, for the first time in years I got some hope a gettin' out of here and stayin' out."

Lawyer Witkin came out to the prison for a meeting with Botchie. After a brief discussion and a detailed description of his meeting with Mr. Banmiller, the lawyer agreed to take the case. Now the days ticked by at a snail's pace for Botchie. He paced about the cell until he about drove Bow Wow crazy. He couldn't sleep and was off his feed. Finally, his cell mate persuaded him to join one of his workout groups. Bowers, who conducted the therapy groups, encouraged Botchie to 'knock himself out' so he'd be able to sleep nights.

At long last Botchie was summoned to Warden Banmiller's office. The expression on the Warden's face telegraphed the expected, bad new. His commutation petition had been denied. "Now, Botchie," the Warden said, "I told you this would happen. But, if you recall, I also said that the petition would almost certainly be granted the second time. Just be patient. Your attorney knows what he's doing.

"This is a big step, Botchie, I'm not only supporting your commutation request, but your lawyer and I are trying to clear all detainers and outstanding sentences. Not only your original sentence of 20 to 40 years, but detainers for all three escapes and the balance of time owed to Sing Sing for parole violation. Everything. When we get this done, you'll be a totally free man!"

Botchie couldn't believe his good fortune. The disappointment of the rejection seemed to disappear, replaced by a lifting of his spirits and the anticipation of release. Now he had to be patient, just as he and Kliney and Saint had been while the tunnel was being built. The daily routine of prison life helped. He kept busy as a block worker, the same job he and Saint had while the tunnel was being constructed. In fact, he passed cell 69 every day. The two inmates locked there were hardly aware of the historic significance of the place. All the men who took part in the escape had gone their separate ways. Even those still inside. Even Sutton, the lying bastard. But, the gang of twelve were all bonded, and always would be.

It was a long wait, nearly two years passed since the commutation process began, but it was worth the wait. One morning, shortly after the second hearing date, Botchie was summoned to the front gate, which meant Banmiller's office. His stomach was tied in knots and his mind awhirl. He tried to push a second rejection from his mind. Funny, before Mr. Banmiller had started this process Botchie hadn't given much thought to being free ever again. It was only after the prospect had been tendered that he started thinking about it. It was nearly all he could think of these days.

When he entered the Warden's office, Botchie knew the outcome. Banmiller's face was masked by one huge, triumphant smile. He grasped Botchie's hand and shook it vigorously and then embraced him as would two athletes, team mates, celebrating a victory. When the Warden finally spoke it was a torrent of words. "Botchie, we got it all–everything. Every year owed, every detainer for escape, even the time for parole violation at Sing Sing."

Botchie had long since collapsed into the chair that was behind him. Had it not been there, he'd have fallen to the floor. Words to express his gratitude failed him. All that came out of his mouth was a repetition of thank you's. Even these small thanks the Warden brushed off. "It has been my genuine pleasure to be able to help you. When you win, I win. If there is anything more I can do, please don't hesitate to call on me."

———————

It seemed that the entire prison population knew about Botchie's good fortune and how Warden Banmiller had provided so much help and support. The House was almost in a celebratory mood, especially during mess when every inmate that could offered congratulations.

For his part, Botchie now had a new set of worries. He thought about his pending new life with some fear and trepidation. *Twenty of the last 33 years I've spent in prison with little short stints on the outside. I have no skills. My new home will be with the Pasha's. Thank heaven for friends. How will I fit in society? Will a good woman have anything to do with me? Hell, I don't even know how to sit and talk to a woman. What's a kiss like . . . ?"*

Mary and Hymie Pasha, long time friends, had arranged for Botchie to be fitted for a new suit, the first he ever owned. "We won't have you leaving that place in prison issue, Jimmy." They offered to come pick him up on the day of his release. Botchie declined with thanks and asked Hymie to pass the word. "Please don't come ta meet me at the gate. I wanna experience walkin' the streets alone."

Botchie and Johnny Bowers, his cell mate and the only close friend he had at the time, said their goodbyes in the cell. Then, dressed in his brand-new suit, Botchie and his friend walked out of 7 Block to the front gate. As the new free man walked through the gate Bowers waved and said. "See ya round."

Chapter 19

The Rest of the Story

Bringing this tale to a satisfactory conclusion means that some effort must be made to describe what happened to all the characters involved. A legitimate question might be which characters? Arbitrarily, it was decided the characters should be those who were part of the tunnel escape. Corvi never was involved in an escape plot and didn't know a thing about any of the escapes until he heard about them on the prison grapevine, the radio. or read it in the newspaper. He's a foil for the other characters, the control case in the story and probably closer to the norm, than guys like Botchie, Sutton and Tenuto. And he knew the people involved in the escapes, some better than others, but he knew them.

Joe and Botchie, friendly acquaintances while in prison, became close friends when both were free. Corvi, at this writing is 85 years old and going strong. Botchie passed away several years ago, but Joe knows his story well. He also came to know Kliney fairly well over the years and kept track of him after he was released. The newspapers tell the story of men like Sutton, BowWow and Bob McKnight. Sutton, of course wrote a book that details his life up to the time of his final release from prison. Of Saint, there is only rumor and conjecture. The rest of the guys: Dave Aiken, James Grace, Bill Szymanski, Bill Russell, Mike Webb and James Simister all represent blank pages. They're like soldiers who fought together in a war, somehow managed to survive and then returned home never to see each other again. At this point, they would be very old men, at least as old as Corvi, and very difficult to track down—if they wanted to be found at all. Here is what is known about some of the characters and their life after prison.

Clarence Klinedinst: Kliney, the real brains behind the tunnel escape from The House, finally received a commutation of his sentence and was released. He went to work as a parking lot attendant on Spring Garden Street in Philadelphia. He may have been able to engineer and construct a tunnel out of Eastern State, but he had trouble navigating the streets of Philadelphia. One day he was struck by a truck while crossing the street and was taken to a nearby hospital for treatment. Upon arriving he was sedated and the next day found that he was the recipient of a new hip–one meant for the patient in the bed next to his. Litigation followed and he was awarded substantial damages. With the proceeds, he bought his first new automobile and was able to live comfortably for the rest of his life. If he had only known the end of the story before embarking on a life of crime, he might have avoided years of prison time.

Fred Tenuto: It was as if Saint disappeared from the face of the earth, never again to be seen. If anybody or any agency really knows, they're not talking–not the FBI, not the Philadelphia or New York City police, not the mafia, and certainly none of his old buddies. However, there are some theories, some rather sketchy-stretchy anecdotal evidence and some rumors.

The incurable romanticists among us suggest that after the Holmesburg escape Saint decided to clean up his act. He and Sutton, it was reported, did at least one job together in New York City that netted them some big money.[1] It would have taken far more than one robbery to finance a permanent retirement. It is supposed that Saint took his share, bid 'adieu' to his breakout pal and headed for parts unknown to start a new life. This *has* happened and, probably, in a few cases successfully, but more often than not escapees and other fugitives from the law are caught sooner or later. None but the diehard romanticists would believe that this is a likely ending to Saint's story.   There are other alternatives.

Remember that Willie Sutton was captured in New York City five years after escaping from Holmesburg with Tenuto and others.   He was fingered by a guy named Arnold Schuster in February 1952.   On March 8, as Schuster was walking home from work, a man stepped out of the shadows and pumped four bullets into him.   He was dead before he hit the sidewalk.   Sutton was in the Queens County House of Correction when the guy who turned him in was killed, gangster style, a couple of blocks from his own home.   The newspapers immediately called Tenuto the murderer. It was a vengeance killing, the code of the underworld in action.[2]

Sutton said, "No way.   Even if there were a code of the underworld, which there isn't, Saint wouldn't have killed Schuster. First, we weren't friends, just acquaintances.   Second, he would have known better than to kill an ordinary citizen.   Third, if he was a friend, he would have known the killing would reflect directly on me and the outcome of my trial."[3]

In the meantime, the police were busy.   The murder weapon was found, discarded in an empty lot located only a few blocks from the murder scene.   The gun, a .38 cal. Smith and Wesson Chief's Special, had been stolen from an Army shipment heading for Japan.   The man who sold the gun identified the buyer as John 'Chappy' Mazziotta.   Mazziotta, a well known hoodlum and bookmaker, hadn't been seen since the day of the murder.   He simply vanished.[4]

So did Tenuto.   He was never seen again, although he remained on the FBI's most wanted list.   In October 1963 his name came up again, this time in the testimony of Joseph Valachi, the notorious and first Mafia informant.   At a United States Senate investigative hearing, Valachi testified that Albert Anastasia, the Mafia boss, had ordered the 'hit' because he was incensed with Schuler's action and his subsequent award of a 'good citizenship' watch.   The man assigned to do the killing was Frederick Tenuto. Anastasia then had Tenuto murdered as well, supposedly to cover his tracks.[5,6]   There was still no sign of Tenuto, in the flesh or otherwise.

Sutton, and a lot of other people at the time, characterized the Tenuto story told by Valachi as stale rumor, gossip, or pure fabrication.[7] There are a lot of questions left unanswered. For instance, why would Saint, a cool and experienced a guy, throw away the murder weapon within a few blocks of the crime and in a place it could easily be found? Why not throw it in the bay or a river or in a garbage dump? Why would Anastasia, however nasty and cold-blooded, order Tenuto killed? That seems an odd thing to do for a man who apparently filled up a grave yard with bodies. After a while he'd run out of people to do his handy work for him.

Joe Corvi thinks the Valachi story is a bunch of bull. In the first place, the man was an informant and not to be trusted. He'd say anything to save his own skin. Secondly, Joe thinks he got the story from the horse's mouth, so to speak.

"Several years following my last release from prison, I was standing in Salerno's Taproom, on the corner of 12th and Moyamensing Ave in South Philly, having a beer. There was an old guy there who I recognized. Never got his name although I knew him to be a member of Mana Nero, The Black Hand, the original Unione Siciliano. I walked over to the old man to pay my respects and offer him a beer, which he accepted. Then we reminisced some about old times.

It turned out the old man was a friend of Saint's father. He remembered the Eastern Pen break when Saint had left via the tunnel. We talked about that for a little while. And he talked about the lack of respect and loyalty among the brotherhood. After a while I asked him a question. Did he believe Saint had made good his escape, that is, was he still alive? That old man looked at me with a knowing smile and said, "Doncha wery." What he meant was, don't you worry. I had my answer.

James Van Sant: Botchie was released from prison in 1959, at age 51, and dedicated the remainder of his life to going straight. He'd definitely had enough of prisons. Besides, he'd taken a vow to never do anything to breach the confidence and trust of Warden Banmiller. After his release, Botchie discovered that a good woman would indeed take him. Within a year he married Ann, whom he met through his friends the Pashas. Another friend, Willie O'Neil (Saint's partner in the Buckeye Club murder of Jimmy DeCaro.) helped Botchie join the Operating Engineers where he worked as a machine operator long enough to earn a generous pension.

All the good behavior after his release didn't erase the shame associated with his life of crime. He confided to his friend Joe Corvi, "Every job I did, I got caught. I was a success at nothin'. My life's story describes 51 years of absolute uselessness–and that's just a bad joke."

Willie Sutton: On Christmas Eve of 1969, at age 68, the State of New York released Willie from Attica. He had served a total of 36 years in prison. After his release, he wrote a book, *Where the Money Was*, occasionally lectured on law enforcement, and spoke at banking seminars on the subject of security. Sutton died in 1980 at 79 years of age. Interestingly enough, ten years earlier Sutton and his lawyer, Katherine Bitses, used the threat of his eminent death to persuade Governor Rockefeller to intervene in a Parole Board dispute. Bitses said, ". . . I'm sure that unless you intervene, the death sentence of the parole board will be carried out for Willie Sutton. . . ."[8] Guess that's why they called him Willie 'The Actor' Sutton.

Horace 'Bow-Wow' Bowers: Bow Wow earned his living as a roofer upon release from prison, about six months after Botchie gained his freedom. He married and bought a home in the Queen Village section of Philadelphia. There he retired, but he never stopped being the tough guy. At age seventy five he was sent back to prison for parole violation. Two young people, Lori Marrandino and Thomas Vargas, were creating a disturbance outside Bowers' home on Bainbridge Street. Bowers' granddaughter went out and asked the party to leave. They didn't. Bowers unlimbered his shotgun, went out to the street and shot Marrandino at very close range, removing a major part of her stomach. Said Bowers, "I'm only sorry I didn't kill the other SOB." Bowers spent the remainder of his life in prison.[9]

Robert McKnight: Upon release in 1956, he opened an ice cream shop on 33rd Street, near Allegheny Avenue in Philadelphia. Two teenagers made it a habit of hanging out on the porch of his store and McKnight objected. One evening, while McKnight swept the sidewalk in front of the store, the boys, Tony Brooks and Samuel Ahmed, came to buy a soda from McKnight's wife. McKnight pulled a gun and held it to Brooks' head. Tony pushed the gun away and told the 70 year-old-man to get out of his face. McKnight shoved the gun to the youth's chest and blasted him. Then the shopkeeper shot Ahmed in the back as he ran away. The charges eventually were dropped.[10]

Joe Corvi: When Corvi was finally released, his wife was the manager of an exclusive women's shop, called Broadway Fashions. His daughter, Jennie, had developed into a lovely young woman. At first, the reunited family moved into an apartment on 12th and Ritner Streets. Later on they purchased a home in Drexel Hill. Joe, not without incident, was reinstated into the Riggers and Machinery Movers Local 161 where he worked for the next 16 ½ years. He retired at age 65. "I always regretted that decision." he said. I loved the work and the people I worked with and the challenges of the job." After retirement Joe, who was in premier physical condition, spent his days either playing racquetball, a game he was quite adept at, or trying to beat the dealers at the blackjack tables in Atlantic City. His rules: Always play against the dealer, not the other players. Never lose any more than the money you arrived with (save enough to return home, of course). Always quit when you've doubled your money or wear out, whichever comes first.

Notes and Sources

I (Steve Conway), for better or worse, am responsible for this book as it appears today. The primary sources for this book are Joseph J. Corvi, the co-author, and James F. Van Sant. Both men were "guests" of the Eastern State Penal System and while their time served overlapped, Van Sant spent far more time inside than Joe. Joe knew Frederick Tenuto beginning with his Huntingdon Reform School experience, but Saint and Corvi were never more than acquaintances. Saint tended to keep to himself, although he and Botchie obviously were pals. All the other characters in this book were acquaintances, with some being closer than others, but none very close at all.

Joe locked in the same cell block as Van Sant and Tenuto at Graterford when the latter two escaped over the wall. Likewise, he was at Eastern State Penitentiary when the famous tunnel escape occurred. In neither case, like most of the inmates at Eastern, was he privy to what was going on until after the fact. He found out like everybody else, through the grapevine or on the news.

Joe was intimately acquainted with all of the institutions in the Eastern Pennsylvania Penal System–Eastern State Penitentiary, Graterford, and Holmesburg–as a result of living or working in all of them. Joe and I spent hours together, at restaurants, my home and on the telephone, with him being interrogated about this man's description, the location of that event, where a certain cell was located, and how that office was furnished.

One of the more interesting experiences, for me at least, was visiting Graterford Penitentiary and the relic of Eastern State, which is now an historic site. Brett Bertolino, Program Coordinator at Eastern State Penitentiary Historic Site, gave Joe, me and my wife, Karen, a guided tour. We visited the cell where Joe locked, Kliney's cell, the entry to the famous tunnel, the segregation unit . . . . All the while we explored this relic of penal philosophy, Joe provided a running commentary–that's the hospital block, here's where I played handball, and this is where Sutton locked. The same thing happened at Graterford where the tour guide was Gerald

Galinski, the Drug and Alcohol Treatment Manager. There have been changes there over the years, but many things remain the same. The quarter mile long main corridor is just as imposing as ever and there are still five cell blocks. Many of the shops are still there, tailor shop, shoe shop and laundry, although functions may have changed some. The yard that Botchie and Tenuto crossed to reach the wall during the Graterford breakout episode is essentially the same. It was interesting that many if not most of the prison personnel at Graterford didn't even know about the escape (Scaling the Wall). Too many years had passed.

It would have been impossible to do a credible job of writing this book without actually seeing the inside of the prisons and having the benefit of Joe Corvi's memories, which remain vivid to this day. But the man who probably helped the most isn't even here to thank. James Van Sant passed away several years ago. The friendship between Joe and Botchie began while they were in prison together, but that relationship didn't really grow until Botchie, at age 51, was released from prison in 1959.

Over time, Botchie and Joe spent more and more time together, mostly at Botchie's Lindbergh Boulevard duplex. Joe drove the twenty minutes to his friend's home and they sat, sometimes in the kitchen having a coffee together and sometimes in the parlor, reminiscing about their days in prison. Joe remembers the attention the two men received from Botchie's small dog. The pet, whose name has long since been forgotten, sat up on the floor between the two men and looked at first one and then the other as the conversation moved from man to man. It was as though the dog was hanging on every word of the stories that passed back and forth. During these long talks Joe learned all of the details about the various escapes, the short intervals of freedom along with Tenuto and others, the long years that Botchie spent in segregation at Eastern State Penitentiary, and many of the men who appear as characters in this book.

Apparently Botchie, along with two other men, began writing a short memoir relating to the 1945 jailbreak from Eastern State at some point after he was released. When Joe Corvi saw it, years ago, it was a manuscript about 50 pages long. While in segregation, after the tunnel escape, Botchie also wrote an epic poem entitled *The Leaking Pen*. The authors attempted to track down these two unpublished documents without success, which is unfortunate. Both would have been very helpful in developing this story.

After Botchie's death Joe began transcribing his memories of their long conversations together. He banged out a rough manuscript of sorts on an old Underwood typewriter, putting in two or three hours a day at the task. That collection of pages, along with hours of conversation, became the basis for this book. In addition, Joe included his own typewritten memories. Since all of the events described occurred so many years ago, one can expect some inaccuracies. However, the basic chronology is correct and is corroborated by numerous newspaper articles, reports and books, all of which are noted among the citations.

The story narrative, including scenes, character development, and dialogue, is naturally based upon Joe Corvi's notes and memories and all the other material available to us. In some cases, scenes were developed as a result of visiting Graterford and Eastern State Penitentiary. Dialogue sometimes represents quotations from published accounts. However, in many cases liberties were taken in the interest of developing the story and making the book more readable. The authors don't apologize for this and hope the reader will appreciate our attempt to reconstruct scenes and dialogue in a way that is at least consistent with the conditions, attitudes, and social expectations of the time portrayed.

SOURCES

Chapter 2
1. "Sutton's Former Prison Pals Waste Little Sympathy on Him."
   Philadelphia Inquirer, February 19, 1952.
2. Ibid.

Chapter 3
1. Willie Sutton with Edward Linn, *Where the Money Was*, The
   Viking Press, New York, 1976, p. 74-75.

Chapter 4

1. Sutton, pp. 73, 85, 114, 115-116.
2. Ibid., pp. 90-93.
3. Ibid., p. 94.
4. Ibid., p. 96.
5. Ibid., p. 98.
6. Ibid., p. 103.
7. Ibid., pp. 109, 116
8. Ibid., p. 122.
9. Ibid., pp. 128-135.
10. Ibid., p. 143.

Chapter 5

1. Norman Johnson with Kenneth Finkel and Jeffrey Cohen, *Crucible of Good Intentions*, Philadelphia Museum of Art, Philadelphia, 1994, p. 80-81.

Chapter 6

1. Johnston, Finkel, and Cohen, p. 89
2. Pete Early, *The Hot House: Life Inside Leavenworth Prison*, Bantam Books, New York, pp. 280-281.

Chapter 7 (Scaling the Wall)

1. Johnston, Finkel, and Cohen, p. 90.

Chapter 8 (A Whole New Life)

1. Susan Weidener, "Advocates in Shock over the fate of MainLine mansion," Philadelphia Inquirer, March 27, 2002, p. B10.

Chapter 10 (There's Always a First Time)

1. Johnston, Finkel, and Cohen, p. 90.
2. Ibid., p. 93.
3. "Rogues Gallery Records of Escaped Convicts," *Philadelphia Inquirer*, April 5, 1945.

Chapter 11 (Moving Up the Ladder)
1. Johnston, Finkel, and Cohen, p. 93.
2. "Eastern Pen Foils Dynamite Plot," *Philadelphia Inquirer*, Philadelphia, December 7, 1944.

Chapter 12 (A Hole at the End of the Tunnel)
1. Nora Pawlaczyk, *Taming the Folklore.*   An unpublished research report prepared for the Eastern State Penitentiary Historic Site. May, 2000, p17.
2. Sutton, p. 183-184.
3. Ibid., p. 184.
4. "Witness Sees Convicts 'Pop Out Like Rats'," Philadelphia Inquirer, April 4, 1945.
5. Ibid.
6. Ibid.
7. Pawlaczyk, p 16.
8. Ibid., 16.
9. "Fugitive Rings Bell at Peniteniary Gate And gives Himself Up; Two Still Missing," Philadelphia Inquirer, April 14, 1945.

Chapter 13 (Freedom is Fleeing)
1. "Last Two Pen Fugitives Planning Bank Holdup When Cought in N.Y.," *Philadelphia Inquirer*, May 23, 1945.

Chapter 14 (The Aftermath)
1. "6 Convicts At Large, 6 Captured." Philadelphia Inquirer, April 4, 1945.
2. "Fleeing Convict Is Shot, 10 Others Trapped in Passage Under Wall." Philadelphia Inquirer, April 3, 1945.
3. "6 Convicts At Large, 6 Captured." Philadelphia Inquirer, April 4, 1945.
4. Gerson H. Lush, "State Orders Probe of Escape," *Philadelphia Inquirer*, April 4, 1945.
5. Johnston, Finkel and Cohen, p. 90.
6. Story as told by Joseph Corvi.
7. Pawlaczyk, p 16.
8. Ibid., p 16.

9. "Fugitive Rings Bell at Peniteniary Gate And gives Himself Up; Two Still Missing," Philadelphia Inquirer, April 14, 1945.

Chapter 15 (Last men at large)
1. The action in New York City is based upon James Van Sant's conversations with Joe Corvi and a news report in the *Philadelphia Inquirer* on May 23, 1945: "Last Two Pen Fugitives Planning Bank Holdup When Caught in N.Y."
2. "Last Two Pen Fugitives Planning Bank Holdup When Cought in N.Y.," *Philadelphia Inquirer*, May 23, 1945.
3. Ibid.
4. Ibid.
5. Ibid.

Chapter 16 (the Crime of Prison Breaching
1. Pawlaczyk, p 16.
2. Johnston, Finkel and Cohen, p. 92.
3. The Leaking Pen was actually written by Botchie, but no copy seems to exist. The authors created the above verses and admit they will win no more prizes than Botchie did.
4. "11 Convicts Refuse to Eat At Pen." Philadelphia Inquirer, October 17, 1945.

Chapter 17 (Notorious Holmesburg)
1. Sutton, p. 192.
2. Ibid, p. 196-209.
3. Ibid., p. 268.

Chapter 19 (The Rest of the Story)
1. "Sutton's Former Prison Pals Waste Little Sympathy on Him," Philadelphia Inquirer, February 19, 1952.
2. Sutton, pp. 246-250.
3. Ibid., p. 250.
4. Ibid., p. 250.
5. Ibid., p. 251.
6. Peter Mass, *The Valachi Papers*, G. P. Putnam's and Sons, New York, 1968, p. 206.

7. Sutton, pp. 253-254.

8. Sutton p. 334.

9. Dave Racher, "BowWow Bowers Heads Back to Jail," *P*
   Philadelphia Daily News, Philadelphia, October 18, 1988, p 16.

10. Kurt Heine, "Storekeeper Warned Teen He Would Kill,"
    Philadelphia Daily News,   Philadelphia, June 26, 1987, p. 34.